Mystery in the Library

By

Mohsen Khabbari

Table of Contents

Dedication i

About the Author ii

Chapter One: Mystery Book 1

Chapter Two: Gate to Other World....................................16

Chapter Three: Forbidden Love 33

Chapter Four: Secret Army 43

Chapter Five: Back in Time 61

Chapter Six: Seven Chamber 80

Dedication

To those who let their inner child free and want to discover more

About the Author

Mohsen Khabbari is a multi-talented, creative person with a passion for storytelling. He started with lifestyle books to help others to reach their goals and solve their problems. These books are "Live the fullest of your life." "Life in the forks" and "God's Elections." Then he started to write a novel to capture readers with unending possibilities.

In the realm of production, he has a visionary approach. From podcasting to photography. He excels in transforming ideas into engaging audio-visual experiences.

Chapter One: Mystery Book

It was 7 minutes after midnight, there was a man named Arthur sitting in the kitchen reading a book. His house was near a grand old library in a small town. The library had tall bookshelves and a quiet atmosphere. It was a wondrous place. The librarian, Miss Adelaide, was a woman of expert knowledge and a twinkle in her eye that hinted at hidden adventures.

There was a young girl who went to live with her grandfather while her parents went on a trip. Previously, Lily had to stay alone in the house when her parents were on the trip, but this time, her parents were worried about leaving her as they did not want to face criticism for being neglectful parents.

One foggy morning, Lily quietly left the house and walked toward the library. As Lily walked through the aisles of books, she felt an instant connection with the library. It felt like she belonged there, and something was calling out to her. The library was filled with the aroma of new books, old ink, and musty pages.

She had no explanation for this, but she felt a wave of calm. It was as if she was floating in the ocean, warm water embracing her body. With a curious nature, she always sought out alternative stories to uncover and solitude was her constant companion. While roaming through the aisles, her attention was captivated by a peculiar book; it was an old dusty book, its cover adorned with faded gold letters. It seemed to beckon her, promising a mystery waiting to be solved.

Lily had heard countless anecdotes over the years about people finding incredible books, rare artifacts, and anything else that involved the paranormal and the unexplained, she just never thought she would get to see it for herself. She was obsessed with the books and already read hundreds of them but this one was different.

She immediately pulled the book from the shelf. On the cover of the book, it said, "The Seal of Solomon" Lily's curiosity was ignited, when she opened it, on the inside of the cover was a handwritten message that read: "Inside this book lies the answers to life's greatest mysteries." she turned the page, the first page was blank, she continued turning page after page but to her awe nothing was written in the pages. Lily's mouth fell open, her jaw was dropped to the floor, and her eyes widened. Perplexed, she approached the librarian, Miss Adelaide, who greeted her with a knowing smile. "Ah, young lady, you have discovered the enchanted book," she said. "Legend says it holds the answers to the greatest mysteries, as well as the deadliest secrets. It has been abandoned for years, and few alive know what awaits anyone who dares to approach it. But only those with a keen mind can unlock its secrets."

After Hours of unsuccessful search, Miss Adelaide approached her and suggested that she come back later that day or tomorrow to search more, and she accepted to leave the library. On the way home, she was thinking about what Miss Adelaide mysteries said.

Suddenly, a barely audible voice said, "The greatest mysteries...life's greatest mysteries..." It was clearly not her imagination. She had heard the voice. Lily's position is secured by a barely detectable, faint voice. She looks around to make sure no one is there. Her eyes were searching for the source of the voice. Lily breathed in deeply. She smelled the aroma of freshly baked cookies.

Ornate and archaic, the scent of countless moldy and dusty tomes filled the air. The taste was similar to peanut butter. The air feels parched and gritty, sticking to the back of Lily's throat like chalky flakes. Her mouth salivated with greed. Her fingers tingle with eagerness to turn each page, and she could taste the mysteries through her mind's eye, each page like a delicacy on her tongue.

"The greatest mysteries," the voice repeated, and this time Lily heard that as if it came from a mysterious creature. It had two red eyes with bluish green irises. It spoke the words in a sibilant whisper, and Lily was certain the creature was speaking to her. The creature vanished suddenly, as if it never existed.

There were numerous layers waiting to be uncovered. Lily's curiosity was so overwhelming she couldn't sleep; instead, she packed her apartment floor. When morning came, she rushed over to the library, searching through aisles to find the book again.

Books of all sizes, colors, and shapes filled the library from floor to ceiling. When she finally found it, she picked up the book and pondered over the book's enigma. As she opened the book something happened, the letters on the pages swirled around and around, rearranging themselves like a Rubik's Cube. Lily staggered backward and threw the book, Lily tried to make sense of the letters. It was then she heard the voice, it was like a whisper in the wind, but it was clear as a bell, free floating letters read, "To reveal the invisible ink, one must expose it to the light of a full moon." Intrigued, she eagerly awaited the next full moon, her mind brimming with curiosity.

When the night of the full moon finally arrived, she sneaked into the library, took the book and went out. The full moon glowed in the sky, its light filling the dark night. Her heart pounded with excitement as the book lay on the ground beneath the branches of the ancient tree on the hill. Illuminated by the moon's ethereal glow, she turned to the first page of the book. To her astonishment, words began to materialize on the previously blank pages, written in a shimmering, invisible ink.

Her eyes widened with excitement as he delved into the secrets hidden within the book's pages. It contained ancient spells, forgotten incantations, and tales of long-lost civilizations. Each page held a new revelation, and she was captivated by the invisible ink's enchanting allure. Watching the secret ink appear, she found joy, like witnessing an age-old magic trick.

As she read on, she noticed a recurring theme. The book was filled with stories of magic and sorcery, but something felt familiar about them. She had heard tales of ancient magic from her grandfather when she was a child, and they bore a striking resemblance to what she was reading. Lily wondered if the stories were true and if they could be used to wield magic in the modern world.

Her eyes fell upon a particularly interesting passage about a spell that could grant incredible power. The spell was dangerous, and not to be taken lightly, but Lily could not resist the temptation. She read the incantation out loud, and a sudden burst of energy shot through her body. She felt as though she could lift a mountain with just one hand.

Lily couldn't believe what had just happened. She had always been fascinated by magic, but she never thought it was real. Now she was holding the key to unlocking its secrets. The book had unlocked a passion within her that she never knew existed. As she closed the book, the words on the page faded away, and the invisible ink disappeared once again. Lily knew that the spell had taken effect, and she felt an inner strength that she had never known before. With her newly acquired power, Lily explored the world around her, she could use her magic for good, and help those in need. Lily's mind raced with the possibilities of what she could do with her newfound power.

As she walked back to her home that night, Lily felt different. It was as if a weight had lifted off her shoulders, and she was filled with a newfound power. She knew that she had to keep the book a secret for fear of being persecuted. But she wanted to explore her powers and see their full potential without thinking about any consequences. The day after, she returned to the library with the book.

Miss Adelaide greeted her and asked if she found what she was looking for? Lily couldn't hold the truth because she was so excited,

Yes, I did. She spoke. It was so incredible... she hesitated to continue. But she continued, you don't believe what happened.

Try me, Miss Adelaide acclaimed.

I brought the book to the full moon, and I could read blank pages, letters were dancing into the thin air, I stepped into the pale light of the full moon, gripping the book in my hands. As I opened it, the illuminated pages seemed to glimmer and glow from within. Letters were suddenly dancing in the air like a flock of birds, forming words and sentences that seemed to carry on an ethereal conversation, Lily added.

Oh, I see, then you must look into it further. Miss Adelaide responded.

Days turned into weeks, and weeks turned into months. Lily continued to experiment with her magic, honing her skills and learning new spells. She discovered that the more she used her magic, the stronger it became. But she also realized that there were consequences to using magic. Every time she cast a spell, she felt a drain on her energy, but she was so excited that she couldn't care less about consequences.one day she met someone who claimed to be master of magic and he was willing to help her to master her craft and powers.

My name is Sam, and I can help you to discover more of your magic, the man said. He revealed to her that when Lily was a little girl; she repeatedly went into another realm, where she learned to wield magic. But her grandfather did something to bind her magic. Now it would make sense that all of the chants and phrases were familiar because she was using them before. The man explained to her that to improve her magic, she could attune it to someone else and use that person's memories as an anchor. She could use that man as her anchor client.

She accepted that, hoping to unravel their secrets and unlock the power of magic with full potential. That man put his hands on Lily's head and murmured something. It seemed that she was drawn into an epic battle between good and evil that had been going on for centuries. She could hear a strange sound of something scratching the floor. Sounds of books being taken off the shelf, or a wooden door creaking open. Confused, she looked around to see where the voice was coming from, but there was no one in sight. Suddenly, she felt an intense gust of wind, and the room began to shake. The shelves started to tremble, and books began to fly off the shelves. Lily quickly realized that she had awakened something dark and powerful with her magic.

The room was filled with an ominous aura, and Lily could feel the presence of something evil lurking in the shadows. Lily's body stiffened, and her skin became covered with goosebumps, as if someone had poured a bucket of ice water over her head.

An ominous shadow emerges, and the room begins to shake. The walls begin to crack and break apart, and the ceiling begins to cave in. She sees a dark figure approaching and a pair of red eyes staring down at her. The shadows moved closer and closer, swirling around her like a tornado, blocking out the light of the room. The shadows cast an ugly veil over her; but it didn't seem to have a shape; they were like a black hole, a vortex of darkness. The shadows were everywhere, like a plague spreading. Her vision was nearly completely black, the only thing she could see was the red eyes staring at her.

The air was thick, like a swarm of bugs had descended upon her. It stuck to her skin, and small wisps of smoke wafted off her body, as if she had been dragged through a fire.the air had become stagnant and rancid, like death and decay. It's as if the shadows had the essence of evil, of pure hatred and disgust. The room is filled with a pungent odor, the smell of rotting filth and mold. She can smell the decay and the stench of death.

The shadows are swirling faster and faster around her, becoming a solid black mass, a dark torment of malice and hatred, grief and pain. She closed her eyes, and she feels as if she can't control her body anymore. She was paralyzed by fear and soon the darkness had a physical presence and texture. She tried to run, but it was as if the air had turned into a thick, viscous substance that was holding her in place. She was trapped and helpless, and the darkness was closing in on her.

The sound of chains clanking together, like a bell ringing out, a chain pulling from a pulley, or a rattle, the sound of the shadows is like nails on a chalkboard, scratching of wood on wood, snakes on a rock. It's the sound of a gale force wind, but there are no windows for one to blow through, and there is no wind howling in the house.

As the shadows move closer, she hears a strange scratching sound, like a crow's foot raking across a wooden barn door. She hears a hollow rattle, a voice speaking in a language she could understand.

Then, out of the darkness, came a figure. It was a hooded figure, shrouded in black robes, with glowing red eyes that pierced through the darkness. Lily could feel the malevolent energy emanating from the figure, and she knew that it was the source of the dark magic.

The figure spoke in a low, raspy voice," I was waiting for this moment for a long time." The air is ripe with the stench of rot and death, of burnt leather and sulphur. Her mouth was dry, and her heart was pounding in her chest.she tastes blood in her mouth and a metallic flavor

in her throat. As the shadows engulfed her, she could taste the blood; it was as if she had become the darkness itself, and it wanted to consume her.

The giant lizard's eyes were the rough and rusty red of fresh blood. But then, something changed. The air around Lily began to shift, and the darkness began to thin. She could feel a warm breeze brush against her skin, and she heard a soft whisper in her ear. It was the voice of Miss Adelaide who had to help her find her magic to fight, and she was urging her to fight back against the darkness that was trying to consume her.

With all her might, Lily closed her eyes and focused on her magic. She could feel it surging within her, like a river that was bursting its banks. She lifted her hands, and a wave of energy shot forth, pushing back the darkness and forcing the hooded figure to retreat.

As the darkness receded, Lily glimpsed the figure's face. It was twisted and grotesque, with features that were almost inhuman. But there was something familiar about it, too. She couldn't place it, but she knew that she had seen it before. With the figure gone, the room began to calm.

She sprinted towards Miss Adelaide, her breath quickening as she arrived. You can't believe what just happened, I was almost consumed by forces of darkness until I heard your voice, and I could get rid of that darkness. "I want to know more about magic "she declared firmly, her voice echoing throughout the room. whispers of lost treasures and forgotten tales echoed through the halls, fuelling her determination.

Ok dear I will help you to do that. Miss Adelaide responded.

With the help of Miss Adelaide, Lily unraveled the secrets of the library's past. The library was a gateway to worlds unknown, a place where mysteries could be the librarian or anyone with the kindred spirit could unravel true magic. The library was a winding path, a place where scrolls and artifacts of many shapes and sizes that'd been collected over time.

Lily and Miss Adelaide explored the library, uncovering secrets from centuries before. The books were filled with stories of places far away, of creatures that Lily had only seen in her dreams. She was captivated by the tales of grandeur and adventure, but even more fascinated by the knowledge contained within them.

As they ventured deeper, Lily realized the sheer magnitude of the library's contents. It was as if a lifetime could be spent studying all the texts and artifacts, yet it still wouldn't be enough to uncover all its secrets.

Suddenly, Miss Adelaide stopped in her tracks. "We have found what we are looking for," she said in a low whisper. She pointed at a small book on the shelf. When Lily opened it up, she found herself staring at the answer to a riddle that had been puzzling her for days: how to open a magical portal into another realm.

Lily stared at the instructions written inside the book, feeling a sense of awe wash over her as she slowly pieced together each step. With Miss Adelaide's help, they gathered all the items needed and positioned them around an archway engraved with strange symbols and runes. Then came what felt like an eternity of waiting until finally something began to happen. A shimmering light shone from within the archway, creating an iridescent bridge between two worlds; two realms that had been separated for so long were now linked together in harmony.

Lily walked through it slowly and cautiously, feeling like she had stepped into another universe entirely with new wonders awaiting discovery around every corner! One of the first things she noticed was a worn wooden chest, marked with an unmistakable symbol, the symbol of the librarians.

It was the site of an old building, but very well preserved. Sunlight filtered through the gigantic windows, leaving dust particles dancing in the air. Miss Adelaide told her that every corner of this library is filled with mystery and magic, and no one could see or touch what is here except the selected one like herself. Inside the wooden chest there was a statue, she touched the statue carved in the image of a warrior, his sword clenched in his teeth. It was cool to the touch, smooth and polished. It was very detailed, like the artist had made it long ago.

There was also an ancient book there, Lily brushed her fingers across the dusty, leather-bound book, and could feel the imprints of the ancient pages beneath her fingertips. Miss Adelaide said: get the book and let's go back. Lily took the book and they came back to the library. Lily asked about that demon and Miss Adelaide answered: there is a battle between good and evil here for centuries, when you trusted that man, you let him overshadow you with dark magic, but you are strong and you could fight it, you just needed a little push or encouragement.

"You are meant for greatness, dear," the old librarian said. "I can sense it in your heart. Follow your heart, and you will find your way. "Lily smiled back, feeling the warmth of the old woman's words. She knew that she had found a genuine friend in Miss Adelaide, and that she would always be grateful for her help in unlocking the secrets of the library. Miss Adelaide said: it is enough for today, leave the book here and come back tomorrow.

With a newfound sense of purpose, Lily left the library, ready to face whatever challenges lay ahead. She knew that there would be dangers and obstacles, but she was ready to face them all with her magic. With the book at her hand she could see more things than ever before.

As she continued to explore the library, Lily could feel the presence of something powerful and ancient. It was as if the books themselves were alive, whispering secrets and ancient knowledge to her. She could see the magic flowing through the shelves and the artifacts, and she knew that she was meant to be here.

There was a corridor behind the shelves of the library and Miss Adelaide asked her to go there, you don't need a light, she stated. It was dark but after a while her eyes adjusted to the dark, everywhere seemed to glow with a cool blue light, radiating their secrets to her. At first it was the same old building that she walked into the other day, but it changed soon,

The new land was breathtakingly beautiful – bright blue skies with clouds like fluffy marshmallows and sunlight glinting off shimmering streams flowing below rugged mountain scape. Butterflies brilliantly danced around wildflower gardens while birdsong filled the air from morning until nightfall when owls took up their serenade under whispering stars above treetops rich with foliage where slumbering pixies frolicked among midnight dewdrops along hidden paths leading out of sight past secret entrances guarded by gargoyles watchful for intruders who might dare come near these ancient lands unseen by human eyes until now thanks to enchanted book of discovery which gifted him this wondrous journey into an uncharted world full of magic.

In the distance, she hears whispers, like the soft rustling or whispering leaves. Suddenly, she heard a voice behind her, a voice that was both ancient and powerful. "Welcome, Lily," the voice said. You successfully open the doors between two realms.

Lily turned around and saw an old man standing before her. He was dressed in a long, flowing robe, and he had a staff in his hand. His eyes were deep and wise, and they seemed to hold a universe of knowledge.

"Who are you?" Lily asked.

The man smiled. "I am the guardian of the Gate," he said. "And I have been waiting for a long time for someone like you to come along. "Lily felt a shiver run down her spine.

After what happened to her with Sam, she couldn't trust anyone, and she asked how do I know you are a real guardian?

The old man's face broke into a warm smile. "I would be happy to answer your question, darling, but the information you seek can only be found in the enchanted book. "He handed over a book and said: look!

The grass swirled around her, and she could smell the scent of night-blooming jasmine, a whiff of dewy earth, and a whiff of night's fresh dew, all teasing her nostrils. Lily reached out her hand and grasped the old man's. "I would do anything to see the book."

She could feel the cool, crisp grass under her toes and fingers. Her skin tingles from the chilly night air. She carefully grabbed the book and turned the page of the book, careful not to invade its privacy, rolled through it with a sea-whiskered voice and unspoken questions hidden within its surf. It was idealistic and passionate, bright and hopeful, a little kitten-like and a little tigress-like. The veil between the present and the past grew thinner, and Lily felt as though she was stepping back in time, experiencing the lives and struggles of those who came before her.

Her power led her down a path that few had ever walked before, uncovering secrets that had been buried for centuries. She delved into the world of the occult, exploring the boundaries of magic and science. She studied ancient alchemy and the esoteric arts, unearthing hidden knowledge that had been lost in the wheels of time. As she delved deeper into the mysteries of the past, Lily felt a sense of purpose grow within her. She knew that she was on the cusp of discovering something truly extraordinary, something that could change the course of history.

Puzzles of the past began to take shape, revealing a tapestry of secrets and long-forgotten narratives. But as Lily ventured further into the depths of history, she began to realize that not all secrets were meant to be uncovered. Some stories were better left buried in the past, their truths too painful to bear. And yet, Lily couldn't help but feel a sense of curiosity and fascination for these hidden tales.

The old man brings her to an old chamber to show her an old parchment. It was not an ordinary piece of paper, with the naked eye you couldn't see anything on it, but Lily saw and read something on that parchment. When she read that it was like somebody rejected a serum of knowledge to her veins. Her eyes shined brilliantly.

Old man asked what did you see. She replied, past knowledge and foundations of the library. The old man asked again: did you notice anything worthy of full attention Lily laughed and asked why?

I wanted to know if you know anything about forbidden love, the old man replied.

Yes, Lily confirmed with a nod. One particular story caught my attention, a forbidden love between a nobleman and an enslaved girl.

The story was shrouded in mystery, its details hidden away in a faded manuscript. Lily knew that this was a story that few had dared to explore, and yet, she felt drawn to its intrigue and forbidden passion. Old man says that is my story, now you know that I am really guardian of the Gate between two realms. But I want to let you know that there is more than one gate between the two realms.I built this library because I wanted to have a safe place in between places.

With a sense of anxiety, Lily delved deeper into the story, her heart racing with anticipation. As she uncovered the hidden details of the romance, she felt her own heart begin to flutter with the thrill of forbidden desire.

Lily's thirst for knowledge was insatiable when she got back to the library she spent countless hours researching and exploring the depths of the library. She was constantly amazed by the hidden treasures that lay within its walls, and each one left her hungry for more.

Chapter Two: Gate to Other World

She spent hours looking every corner of the library, searching for hidden messages and clues. Although she couldn't find anything written on pages but with further exploration, she was thinking about what that man told her about there being more than one gate between two realms. She found more secrets hidden within the library behind the bookshelf.

One day she was reading a book looking for a mystery to solve, she got distracted by the sound of a fairy. She could hear the flapping of wings and the gust of wind howled as it blew through the open window, blotting out the sound of her own breathing.

She was a real, tiny lost fairy named Sparkle. Sparkle had lost her magical powers and couldn't find her way back home. Lily knew she had to help her new fairy friend. Determined, she asked Sparkle how she could assist. Sparkle explained that she needed to find a special flower called the Glow berry to regain her powers. The Glow berry could only be found deep within the Enchanted Forest. The address of the place was written in the book with invisible ink.

Lily carefully examined all the shelves, hoping to find a clue that would help them on their quest. Finally, Lily found the book with the clue they needed. Using her magic, she revealed the hidden words: it was written "Seek the tree with the glowing bark, and there you shall find the Glow berry."

With a sense of excitement and anticipation, she raced back to Sparkle with the information they needed to find the Glow berry. Now they had to find the door to the magical realm, sparkle rummaged through her pocket and pulled out the hard, smooth glass vial in which she kept the portal to the magical realm. It was not too big for her to hold in one hand, but it could open a portal large enough for them to pass through.

The two friends set off on their adventure, braving the dangers and obstacles that lay ahead. She cautiously walked through, unsure of what she would find on the other side. As they passed through the mysterious doorway, a chill crept up Lily's spine as she realized that they had stepped into another realm. The door led to an ancient stone wall that seemed to stretch for miles in all directions. Which was engraved with strange symbols. Following an instinct, Lily placed her hand against the wall and whispered a magical incantation. Instantly a door appeared, revealing a secret passage leading even deeper into this magical realm.

To her surprise, the corridor opened up into a lush, magical world filled with towering trees and sparkling rivers. Lily stepped out of the secret corridor, into a world unlike any other. The lush green trees towered above her, the morning dew giving them a brilliant sheen in the bright sunlight. A soft breeze rustled through the leaves, carrying with it the gentle chirping of birds and the tinkling sound of distant laughter.it was a realm filled with magic and mystery. She realized that the book held more than just mystical secrets; it held the key to a hidden world right behind the library.

The two adventurers made their way down long winding tunnels until finally arriving at a vast chamber covered in glowing runes and decorated with flowing vines and twinkling stars. In the center of this chamber stood an imposing tree whose bark glowed like fireflies in the night sky.

Excitedly, they rushed forward, only to find that there were no berries on the tree. They realized that if they wanted to get the Glow berry back to Sparkle's home, they would have to find another way. With Sparkle perched happily on her shoulder, Lily made her way down a winding path that led deeper into the forest.

As they made their way further in, Lily noticed a faint light coming from deep within a thicket of trees. She motioned for Sparkle to follow her as she crept closer towards it. As they drew nearer, Lily realized that it was coming from an enormous tree with glowing bark.

She knew that this was the place they were looking for, after hours of searching, they reached a clearing where they saw a giant tree with glowing bark. Lily and Sparkle knew this was what they were looking for -the Glow berry tree! She slowly reached out to touch it, and suddenly she felt a magical surge flow through her veins.

Everywhere around them were signs of life; from brightly coloured butterflies fluttering past to mischievous foxes peeking from behind bushes. It was here, amidst this enchanted landscape, that Lily found what she was looking for, the Glow berry tree!

The air crackled with an energy Lily had never felt before, they journeyed deep into the heart of the Enchanted Forest, following a narrow path that wound its way through the dense foliage. Home of the Glow berry! She recognized it immediately with its glowing bark, shimmering leaves and delicious looking berries that hung from its branches.

With trembling hands, she plucked a few and held them in her cupped palms for Sparkle to see. "We found it!" she exclaimed excitedly, feeling a rush of accomplishment course through her veins.as they walked, Lily could feel the magic of the forest seeping into her bones. The trees whispered secrets to her, and the flowers bloomed with brilliant colors and scents that she had never seen or smelled before. She knew that she was in a place of great power, and she felt her own magic growing stronger with each step.

As she searched, she couldn't shake off the feeling that they were being watched. A sense of danger hung heavy in the air, and she knew that they needed to be careful.

As they continued on their path, they encountered many obstacles along the way, such as thorny vines blocking their path and dark creatures lurking in the shadows. Treacherous paths to ferocious beasts. But they persevered, driven by their determination and help of friendly woodland creatures like squirrels and rabbits, who happily pointed them in the right direction to help Sparkle regain her powers.

Suddenly, Lily heard a voice inside her head telling her about a secret entrance that would lead them to an underground cavern. She chased these directions and eventually arrived at a small opening in the ground that led into an underground tunnel system.

With Sparkle on her shoulder, she made her way deeper into the cave and they stumbled upon a glimmering chamber filled with wonder and mystery. The chamber was lined with crystals that glowed brightly in the dark.

As Lily stepped further into this wondrous place, she felt an undeniable presence inside - it seemed as if some kind of powerful force was watching over them. With Sparkle perched on her shoulder, Lily stared up at what stood before her: a being so glorious yet mysterious, shrouded in layers of mist that crackled with electricity! Its gaze weighed heavily on her soul, even though its face remained hidden from sight. She instinctively knew this entity held great power;

perhaps even greater than her own magic abilities, magical opportunities for those brave enough to seek it out!

Little did Lily know; she had reached the court of the magical Guardians of The Forest. Standing before them was an awe-inspiring sight; three dazzlingly beautiful creatures that introduced themselves as Dason, Malena and Eleocharis wearing exquisite gowns made from rare and enchanted materials. Dazzling enchantments filled their eyes as they stepped forward in unison to greet her with open arms.

Lily was amazed by the beauty and power of the Guardians. They shared with her secret knowledge that flowed through every living creature and connected us all. She understood that a significant source of magic was present in this place, but they also warned her that such power could be dangerous if abused.

The Guardians then proceeded to give Lily some powerful words of protection, incantations for her to use on their journey ahead. They told her to repeat these incantations whenever she felt threatened or scared for her life, as it would ensure her safety from any evil forces that may cross her during the quest.

The three Guardians then instructed Lily and Sparkle to seek out the four hidden Wonders of Nature - Earth, Wind, Fire and Water - in order to restore Sparkle's powers. As they prepared for their quest ahead, the Guardians offered one ultimate piece of advice: remember that only those who are brave enough can succeed in this task.

With a newfound determination and courage, Lily and Sparkle waved goodbye to The Guardians and set off on their journey. Knowing they had been blessed with knowledge beyond what most possess made them feel invincible even though danger lurked around each turn. Together they walked forward into the unknown, determined to restore balance to the land before it was too late!

From then onwards, Lily knew they'd never truly be alone as long as nature walked beside them,the glittering stars in the sky reminding what strength could come when unity between good is formed!

With the Glow Berry safe in hand, they returned to Sparkles home world carefree and victorious! Overjoyed, Sparkle thanked Lily for her help and said she has to go alone to find four hidden Wonders of Nature but first she first offered to take her to the fairy kingdom. Lily accepted,

After a while, they finally entered the entrance of the Fairy kingdom, with its shimmering trees and glowing flowers. Excitement filled the air as Lily and Sparkle stepped into the magical realm.

As soon as they entered, Tinker Bell welcomed them and asked what she could do for them. Her tiny wings fluttered in excitement. "Do you want to see something truly magical?" she asked. Lily and Sparkle nodded eagerly, and Tinker Bell led them to a hidden glade in the heart of the forest. There, under the light of a thousand fireflies, they witnessed a towering castle made entirely of crystal with walls that sparkled like diamonds in the sunlight. She knew in her heart that this was where she was meant to go. They traveled to the center of the kingdom, and they found a cottage with a chimney which was brown with brick. Lily knocked at the door and an old wise guy opened the door; his name was Lockwood, he came out and said, what brings you to this place? Lily explained how they managed to help sparkle find her way back home. And she wants to go find four hidden wonders.

It is the start of your journey, wise man said, let me tell you a story. When you go back, remember this story.

Once upon a time, in a quaint little town nestled amidst rolling hills, there lived a young man named Arthur. He was known for his vivid imagination. One day, while strolling through a dusty old bookstore, he stumbled upon a peculiar book titled "The Invisible Book."

Intrigued by its mysterious title, Arthur gingerly picked up the book and began to read. To his astonishment, the pages were completely blank. Confused yet fascinated, he turned the pages, hoping to uncover the secret behind this invisible book. Suddenly, words began to materialize before his eyes, as if ink was magically appearing on the pages.

Lily was shocked and interested when he heard the story because she also has found a book with invisible ink.

He bought the book and showed it to his parents, but they reproached him, and they said you are wasting your money, with the book at hand, he discovered he possesses the extraordinary ability to see things that were invisible to others. He was reading the book and was obsessed with the book. After finishing the book, he read it again and again.

As Arthur delved deeper into the story, he realized that the book was not just a mere collection of words, but a portal into a world where the invisible became visible, he could see the wind whispering through the trees, the laughter of fairies dancing in the moonlight, and even the dreams that floated above people's heads.

He found a magic that he could write whatever wanted in the book and it became reality. Unable to resist the allure of this invisible book; he started to write in the book whatever he wanted.

People marveled at the author's ability to bring such a fantastical concept to life. He became a famous writer, and he could capture readers from all walks of life.

The invisible book had opened his eyes to a world he had never truly seen before. Years passed, and Arthur continued his writing and traveled to another world. He wanted something more, he could be transported to a realm where imagination knew no bounds and where the power of words could shape reality and it was so, he gained the knowledge of writing with an invisible book and with his writing he could be transported from reality to another realm. But it was not enough for him.

"Do you think that it's possible for someone to gain the power to transport themselves to another realm just by writing?" she asked Lockwood.

"It's possible," Lockwood replied with a nod. "Writing has the power to unlock hidden potential within a person. It allows us to explore and create worlds beyond our own, and in doing so, we open ourselves up to new possibilities and experiences."

Lily was fascinated by the idea, and she couldn't wait to try it for herself. She knew that she had a lot to learn, but with Lockwood's guidance, she was confident that she could harness the power of the invisible book, just like Arthur had.

Lily nodded in understanding. She listened to Lockwood's story with rapt attention, feeling as though she too had been transported to another world. She couldn't help but wonder if the book she had found possessed a similar magic. Perhaps, like Arthur, she too could unlock a new world of possibilities.

Can I do it, can I do it now? Lily asked?

Lockwood smiled, sensing the young girl's curiosity. "It's possible," he said, "Anything is possible if you allow yourself to believe. "Remember, with great power comes great responsibility," he cautioned. "Be careful what you write, for words have the power to shape reality itself." "But the story hasn't finished yet. He reached to the point that he wants to use the invisible book for his own benefit. So, he got money from people and wrote what they wanted. They could go on a trip to where they wanted, and they could come back as long as they paid Arthur. As word of the invisible book spread, people from all walks of life yearned to experience its magic. The legend of Arthur's masterpiece grew. However, not everyone had noble intentions. A cunning thief named Sam Karner, notorious for his love of rare artifacts, set his sights on the book. Determined to possess its secrets, he hatched a plan to steal it from Arthur's study. He wanted to have the original copy. Under the cover of darkness, Sam crept into Arthur's house, his eyes gleaming with greed. He snatched the book from its resting place and made his escape. As Sam opened the book, eager to uncover its secrets, there was nothing in the book, only blank pages.

He was confused and frustrated. How could a book with such a legendary reputation be blank? Was it a fake? But he couldn't shake the feeling that there was something more to this invisible book. He spent days poring over the blank pages, trying to decipher any hidden messages or clues.

The book could only be read by someone who had pure intentions and a genuine desire to explore the invisible. Sam, blinded by his greed, could never have access to the book's magic. As he threw the book away in frustration, he unknowingly threw away Arthur's chance at discovering a world beyond his wildest imagination.

Disappointed and angry, he threw it away. Sam couldn't believe that the book that had caused so much hype was nothing but a scam. He thought that he had wasted his time and resources on something that was worthless, and cursed Arthur for his deceit. He threw it away in the street. Arthur discovered that his book was stolen, so he tried his magic to track the book, but he realized he had lost his powers, little did he know that there was more to the book than met the eye. The invisible ink that Arthur had used to write the book had faded over time, making the pages look blank. When Arthur misuses the book's power, he attracts people like Sam who want to use the magic power for the dark side, then its power transfers to someone else.

That was the story I wanted to tell you, let me give you final advice, pay attention to the story I just told you and you can find four wonders in the middle of the pages in the library. Lily was astonished by the story, asked, what happened to Arthur and how the story ends? Arthur lived happily without magic power also and there was no end to this story, the wise man replied.

As they parted ways, she was thinking about the story she had heard, and returned to the library. Armed with her new knowledge, Lily decided to explore beyond what she had seen so far. She knew that behind each of those bookshelves lay secrets waiting to be discovered secrets that could change her life forever.

Book was in the street for days until a young girl found it. Her name was Madalyn Adelaide, when she found the book, it caught her eyes because the book was glowing in blue. She went home and opened the book, pages were blank, but it didn't take long, the room began to shimmer and warp, and suddenly, she found himself transported to a different realm.

It was a place unlike anything he had ever seen before, a world of magic and wonder, filled with strange creatures and otherworldly landscapes. And there, in the distance, she saw the most incredible sight, a magnificent castle that towered towards the sky, its turrets and spires glinting in the light of a setting sun.

Without hesitation, Madelin set off towards the castle, her heart pounding with excitement and wonder. As she approached, she was greeted by a group of friendly fairies who welcomed her with laughter and song.

"Madelin, welcome to the fairy kingdom," they said. "We have been expecting you."

Madelin was shocked by their greeting, but she felt a sense of belonging amongst the fairies. They led her through a vibrant forest, filled with glowing plants and creatures. As she made her way towards the crystal castle, she couldn't help but marvel at the beauty of this new world. It was as if everything was alive and pulsing with energy, from the shimmering trees to the glittering streams. Never knew existed. Finally, they arrived at the grand entrance of the castle.

"Madelin, you possess a rare gift, the power of the invisible book. Only a select few have ever held this power, and you are one of them." One fairy told Madelin.

Finally, she arrived at the castle's main hall and was met by a group of fairies who greeted her with smiles and laughter. They led her through the castle's winding corridors and up a spiral staircase until they reached a grand hall filled with shimmering crystals.

There, she saw a figure clad in robes of pure white, with a staff in hand and a kind smile on her face. It was the old wise woman looking like a queen, and she had been waiting for her. "Madelin," she said, her voice soft and gentle. "Welcome to the Crystal Kingdom. We have been expecting you.

The library was a gateway to worlds unknown, one evening, as the moon cast an ethereal glow upon the library, Lily stumbled upon a hidden passage behind a bookshelf. With bated breath, she followed the winding path, her heart pounding with anticipation. The passage led her to a hidden chamber filled with ancient artifacts and dusty tomes. Among the relics, Lily found a worn journal that belonged to an old librarian. Its pages were filled with cryptic notes and sketches, hinting at a hidden treasure buried beneath the library. Determined to solve the mystery, Lily deciphered the clues and embarked on a thrilling adventure.

She followed the clues, which led her through the twisting corridors of the library and down into its deepest depths. There, she found a hidden door, and behind it, a staircase that descended into darkness.

As she walked down the stairs, Lily could feel her heart racing fast. What would she find at the bottom of this hidden passage? As she reached the bottom, she saw a faint light flickering in the distance. She got closer to see better; the light grew brighter until she found herself standing before an enormous chamber filled with glittering jewels and golden artifacts. In the center of the room, there was a pedestal upon which rested a glowing orb.

With trembling hands, Lily reached out and touched the orb. Suddenly, she was struck by a blinding light, and she felt herself being lifted off the ground. When the light faded, she was standing before a group of wise old librarians.

There, she saw a figure clad in robes of pure white, with a staff in hand and a kind smile on her face. It was the queen, and she had been waiting for her.

Lily, she said, her voice soft and gentle. "Welcome to the Crystal Kingdom. We have been expecting you."

You are selected to use magic for the greater good and pass it onto the next generation. You are destined to do great things. As you know, with great power comes great responsibilities, let me start off your journey with the task of knowing the library well. You should get back to the library and get yourself familiar with all the books.

When she returned to the library, Miss Adelaide asked, I see that you got your first task.

How do you know? Lily asked.

Because your eyes are glowing, Miss Adelaide responds.

I had an amazing trip to another realm, and I heard a story about Arthur and Madeline and at last I met the counsel of librarians.

I see, Miss Adelaide said. You have enough knowledge to start your task, I can help you.

I am wondering what happened to Arthur or Madelaine? Lily asked.

She smiled, let me help you with that, Miss Adelaide replied.

Did you find a worn journal filled with cryptic notes and sketches? Miss Adelaide added.

How do you know that? Lily asked with astonishment.

I know it because it is my journal, Miss Adelaide responds.

Lily's mouth fell open, her jaw was dropped to the floor, and her eyes widened. It was then she remembered the voice. It was like a whisper in the wind, but it was clear as a bell.

She remembered, when she was fighting with darkness, she heard a voice which was Miss Adelaide's voice. She let out a low gasp of surprise.

My name is Madelaine Adelaide, and I am the girl who found the book after Arthur lost his powers. But you must find out about Arthur yourself, it is not my secret to tell you. Miss Adelaide added.

Lily had no explanation for this, but she felt a wave of calm. It was as if she was floating in the ocean, warm water embracing her body.

You will be the new librarian here and give her a book, start with this book and you can read the journal, I am glad that you found it. Lily glanced around the library, taking in the large shelves of books and the scent of aged paper. Miss Adelaide motioned for her to approach with a low, beckoning voice. Lily stepped forward and Miss Adelaide handed her an old book; its pages were yellowed from years of use and Lily could feel the texture of the worn leather cover beneath her fingertips.

With the help of Miss Adelaide, Lily unraveled the secrets of the library's past. They followed a trail of clues that led them through secret tunnels and hidden compartments until they finally reached the heart of the mystery. Beneath the library, there was a hidden treasure trove, filled with precious artifacts and forgotten stories.

As Lily and Miss Adelaide dug deeper into the treasure trove, they uncovered an ancient map that hinted at the location of a legendary artifact said to possess immense power and wisdom. The map was filled with cryptic symbols and obscure writings, but Lily's sharp mind and intuition allowed her to decipher its secrets; it was a first draft of "seal of Solomon."

Lily and Miss Adelaide had a tiresome journey ahead of them, but they were determined. During their discoveries, they encountered mysterious strangers who sought to disrupt their mission and take the artifact for themselves. However, with clever strategies and quick thinking, Lily and Miss Adelaide managed to outsmart their foes each time.

Eventually, after weeks of travel, they arrived at their destination: a long-forgotten temple hidden deep in the desert. As they entered the temple's courtyard, Lily could feel an ancient power radiating from the walls. After navigating through a series of treacherous puzzles and traps, the duo finally reached the inner chamber where the artifact was said to be hidden.

Miss Adelaide pulled out her ancient map one last time and used it to guide them towards a secret door in the back of the chamber. With trembling hands, she opened it up to reveal an old wooden box containing a small metal object: The Seal of Solomon! This time not the book, but the seal itself.

The seal felt incredibly heavy in Lily's hand as she lifted it up; it was shiny, almost as if it was made from pure gold instead of metal. She looked over at Miss Adelaide who had tears streaming down her face, not only had she fulfilled her lifelong quest but also found something far greater than she ever imagined: A legacy that will live on for generations to come.

The artifact, a mysterious amulet, lay hidden within a labyrinthine cave system guarded by fierce beasts and deadly traps. Undeterred, Lily and Miss Adelaide pressed forward, their hearts filled with determination and courage. As they reached the heart of the cavern, they found the amulet shimmering with an otherworldly glow.

Each layer they peeled back revealed an additional dimension, the historical context alone provided a rich tapestry of events and influences that shaped the topic's evolution. Delving into the complexity of the subject, each contributing to a deeper understanding. The more Lily immersed herself in the subject, the more she realized the significance it held not only in the past but also in the present. It became evident that this exploration was not just about understanding the historical context; it was about unraveling the threads that connected the past to the present, and ultimately shaping the future.

As she continued her research, she found herself drawn deeper into the labyrinth of historical records. Each page she turned revealed an extra layer of complexity, urging her to delve further into the depths of knowledge. It seemed an unending discovery. The subject had transcended a mere intellectual pursuit; it had become a personal quest for understanding and enlightenment. With each revelation, she felt a renewed sense of awe and reverence for the countless individuals who had shaped our world.

As she delved deeper into the archives, her eyes were met with a treasure trove of forgotten stories and hidden truths. The dusty manuscripts and faded photographs whispered tales of triumph and tragedy, of ordinary individuals who had left an indelible mark on the tapestry of history. Each artifact held a piece of the puzzle, a fragment of a larger narrative waiting to be uncovered. With every discovery, her excitement grew, fuelled by the realization that she had the power to resurrect these voices from the depths of obscurity. Among these, there was something special, a parchment. Lily took it and they returned to the library.

Chapter Three: Forbidden Love

Lily stared at the ancient parchment in awe, her mind was racing with curiosity and excitement. The words "The Seal of Solomon" echoed in her head, triggering a flood of questions. What could this seal be? Who was Solomon? And why was it mentioned in this mysterious document?

According to ancient texts, this seal held immense power and served as a key to unlock hidden knowledge and control supernatural entities. It was believed to grant its bearer authority over demons and forces of darkness, enabling them to perform incredible feats.

Each symbol and cryptic writing held the potential to unlock a world of untold power and wisdom. The weight of responsibility pressed upon me, reminding me of the countless lives that could be affected by the knowledge I sought. With every passing moment, my determination grew stronger, fuelled by the realization that this quest was not just for personal gain, but for the greater good of humanity. She knew that the challenges ahead would be daunting, but she was prepared to face them head-on. With renewed resolve, she delved deeper into the enigma of the Seal of Solomon, ready to uncover its secrets and fulfill her destiny.

Everything she found was a piece of the puzzle. She completed her knowledge of the magic realm and also gave her another kind of magic power, with every knowledge comes new power and new responsibility.

With newfound confidence and determination, Lily vowed to continue her quest for knowledge and adventure. She knew that the path ahead would not be easy, but she was ready to face any challenge that came her way. As she left the hidden chamber and returned to the library's familiar halls, she felt a sense of excitement and purpose fill her heart. For Lily, the library had transformed from a quiet sanctuary to a place of endless possibility and adventure. She was eager to dive into the dusty tomes and explore every hidden nook and cranny. She was no longer a mere visitor, but a fearless explorer, fuelled by the thrill of discovery and the promise of untold treasure.

As her journey continued, Lily found herself drawn deeper into the labyrinth of history, her mind consumed by the mysteries and untold stories that lay waiting to be uncovered. She spent long nights poring over ancient manuscripts and tomes, her eyes tracing the intricate symbols and cryptic writings.

As Lily ventured further into the depths of history, she began to realize that not all secrets were meant to be uncovered. Some stories were better left buried in the past, their truths too painful to bear. And yet, Lily couldn't help but feel a sense of curiosity and fascination for these hidden tales.

She came across again a forbidden romance between a nobleman and an enslaved girl. Lily knew that this was a story that few had dared to explore, and yet, she felt drawn to its intrigue and forbidden passion.

With a sense of fear, Lily delved deeper into the story, her heart racing with expectation. As she uncovered the hidden details of the romance, she felt her own heart begin to flutter with the thrill of forbidden desire. The noble man's devotion to the enslaved girl was both heartwarming and tragic, as their love was forbidden by society's strict rules. Lily couldn't help but feel a sense of admiration for their bravery and determination to love each other despite the odds. With a sense of purpose, Lily set out to unravel the mystery of the forbidden romance. She spent countless hours poring over old manuscripts and dusty tomes, her mind consumed by the tales of love and loss. And yet, the more she uncovered, the more she realized that the story was more than just a tale of forbidden love. It was a window into a time and place that was both beautiful and tragic, filled with stories of hope.

As Lily continued to read, she became more and more engrossed in the story. She felt as if she were living in a different world, surrounded by the sights and sounds of a bygone era. The story called to her, igniting a sense of passion and desire that she couldn't ignore.

With each word she read, Lily's heart raced with excitement and longing. She found herself lost in the forbidden romance, imagining herself as the enslaved girl, swept away by the nobleman's undying devotion. Her mind was consumed by thoughts of passion and desire, and she couldn't help but yearn for the same kind of love that the couple had shared.

Lily's longing grew more intense, so jumped into the story. She found herself fantasizing about the nobleman, imagining his muscular arms holding her close, his lips pressing against hers in a fiery kiss. Her body trembled with desire, and she knew that she could not resist the temptation any longer. She could feel love and strength from both of them.

Both of whom had defied societal norms to pursue their love. The more she learned about their struggles and triumphs, the more she yearned to experience their passion for herself. She knew that she shouldn't be feeling this way, that it was wrong to let her desires consume her, but she couldn't resist the pull of the story.

As the nights wore on, Lily found herself fantasizing about the nobleman and the enslaved girl. She imagined herself in the girl's place, surrendering to the nobleman's touch and feeling the heat of his passion. She knew that it was just a fantasy, that she could never act on her desires, but she couldn't help but feel a sense of longing.

One evening, while she was deep in her thoughts, Lily felt a hand on her shoulder. She jumped, startled, and turned to see Miss Adelaide standing behind her.

"Lily, my dear, are you alright?" Miss Adelaide asked, concern was all over on her face.

Lily could feel her cheeks flush with embarrassment as she realized how lost in her thoughts she had been. She quickly composed herself and nodded, smiling weakly at Miss Adelaide.

"I'm fine, just lost in thought, "Lily replied, trying to brush off her inappropriate fantasies.

Miss Adelaide gave her a knowing look, as if she could sense what Lily had been thinking. "I understand, my dear. The stories in this library have a way of consuming us. But remember, some stories are better left untold."

Lily nodded, feeling a sense of shame wash over her. She knew that Miss Adelaide was right, but she couldn't shake off the passion and desire that the forbidden romance had ignited within her.

As she left the library that night, Lily couldn't help but feel conflicted. Part of her wanted to continue exploring the depths of history and uncovering the mysteries of the past, but another part of her was consumed by the forbidden desires that had been awakened within her. She knew that she needed to find a way to reconcile these conflicting feelings and make peace with the past.

Over the next few days, Lily tried to focus on her studies and research, putting the forbidden romance out of her mind. But no matter how hard she tried; she couldn't shake off the intense desire that had consumed her. She felt as if she were living a double life, one in which she was the studious and curious librarian, and another in which she was the passionate and forbidden lover.

One day, as she was fantasizing again about a nobleman, Lily heard a knock on her door. She opened it to see the nobleman from the forbidden romance standing before her, his eyes burning with desire.

"Lily," he shouted her name, "I have come for you. Lily stared at the nobleman in disbelief. She had never expected to see him in her own home, much less standing right outside her door. She stepped back, allowing him to enter her room without a word. He seemed to take up the entire room with his presence, Lily could feel her heart racing as he closed the door behind him. The rustling of his tattered cloak filled the air as he ran toward where she stood. "I believe that we have unfinished business," he said simply, and Lily felt a shiver run down her spine as she realized what he was implying. The nobleman stepped closer, his gaze full of unspoken desire, come with me, Lily accepted. When they went out together, there was no ordinary world. A twinkling array of stars glittered in the sky, while traffic and city lights were nowhere in sight. There was another world out there, and no sign of that nobleman.

Lily blinked, wondering if she had been dreaming, but the world around her remained unchanged. She shook her head, trying to clear her thoughts, but the desire and longing remained.

Lily's face fell and her eyes filled with disappointment for a moment because there was no nobleman there, but she could manage herself and looked around to see what was there.

She knew that she should be excited that she was in a new world, but a part of her couldn't help but feel a sense of disappointment. She knew that it was foolish, that she could never act on her desires, but the pull of the forbidden romance was too strong to ignore.

She took a deep breath and tried to calm herself down. She knew that she had to be rational and figure out what was happening. As she looked around, she realized that she was in a different world, far removed from the library where she had spent most of her time.

The world was different, but not completely alien to her. It was a place of magic and wonder, filled with creatures that she had already met or read about.

Suddenly, she heard a voice behind her. "Lily, my darling, are you alright?"

She turned around, expecting to see the nobleman again, her eyes filled with wonder, but this time she saw an old wise woman. She felt a powerful surge of desire and longing as she whispered her name again.

Lily hesitated, unsure of what to do!

I see you are confused, an old wise woman said with a smile.

Lily was aware that she had to devise a plan to harmonize her conflicting emotions. Lily stood in shock, her heart racing with a mixture of fear and desire. She couldn't believe what was happening, was it real or was it just a figment of her imagination, a product of her own forbidden desires?

Lily blinked, trying to make sense of the situation. As she looked closer at the person in front of her, she realized that she was the queen that had met her before.

Lily's thoughts spun out of control as she struggled to comprehend what was happening.

The room was filled with the smell of jasmine. A briny, pungent smell of salt water filled the air. Lily noticed that she could smell the salty air on the woman's clothes. The air was damp and redolent with the scent of moss and pine.

The floor beneath her feet was smooth and cool, made of soft marble. She felt the worn wooden floorboards against her feet. The air was crisp, making her hair stand on end in the gusting wind.

Lily's head felt a light feeling of dread passed over her, and she worried that she might faint. The images of the skies she had seen earlier had vanished, replaced with the long hallway. The wise woman was looking at her with a look of concern. Her eyes were sea-gray, and her hair was a golden color, streaked with white.

The hallways were dark, with flickering torches every few feet, and long arched windows every few feet. Lily heard the sound of footsteps behind her as she slowly walked down the hall.

The Queen said: don't be afraid, I am here to help you.

Lily felt a sense of relief wash over her as she realized that the nobleman was not a figment of her imagination, but a real person who had come to her aid. She took a deep breath and tried to compose herself.

"I'm sorry," she said, "I'm just feeling a little overwhelmed. "Lily inhaled deeply and caught a whiff of stale sweat, old pipe smoke, and musty leather.

The old woman smiled kindly at her. "I understand, my dear. This world can be quite overwhelming at first. But don't worry, I am here to help you."

Lily felt the rough texture of the stone floor beneath her bare feet. She looked down and saw that she was wearing a white peasant's dress.

A few other men and women all dressed white appeared beside the queen.

"Young one," the queen spoke again, "You have been chosen to carry on our legacy. Our love was once forbidden, but now it is your turn to break the barriers and live freely."

Lily felt a wave of excitement and fear wash over her. Could she really carry on their legacy? Could she find the strength to fight for love in a world that still frowned upon it?

She continued reading the parchment. Man's love for the enslaved girl was intense and all-consuming, but it was also forbidden by society's strict rules. Lily could feel their passion and pain within the faded page, as if their love had transcended time itself. As she read on, Lily realized that the story had a good ending. Although the nobleman was forced to abandon his love, who was then sold into slavery and never seen again, she became queen's favorite servant and after the queen died she became queen herself. Lily felt an intense sadness and heartbreak, realizing that their love had been stamped out by a cruel and unforgiving world. But despite the tragedy, Lily felt a sense of relief because the enslaved girl now is a queen. Their love had been pure and powerful, but it never worked because of the constraints of society. Lily knew that their story would stay with her forever, a testament to the enduring power of true love and human resilience.

Lily spent the next few days exploring the new and exciting world she had stumbled into, one of the old wise men of the counsel guided her around, showing her the wonders of this new land and introducing her to the different creatures that inhabited this land. She learned about the different creatures that inhabited the world from the mischievous fairies to the fierce dragons. She was in absolute awe of all the creatures she met. She even learned how to talk to an unfamiliar creature, something that had always been a fantasy of hers.

Lily was amazed at how quickly she picked up these new skills. She had always wanted to know what it would be like to wield such power, and now here she was doing just that!

The old wise man smiled encouragingly as he watched Lily test out her newfound abilities. He knew that she would make a great addition to their realm.

One evening, when they stopped for the night, the old wise man suggested they take a break in a nearby clearing among some tall trees. As Lily sat beneath them, looking up at the twinkling stars above her head, she felt an odd sense of peace come over here.

It was then that Lily made a vow, no matter what came her way in life, she would use her power for good and fight for love wherever possible. She knew that this was an enormous responsibility but also an incredibly exciting one, and with her newfound confidence; she felt ready for whatever challenges lay ahead!

Despite the excitement and wonder of this new world, Lily couldn't help but feel a sense of longing and yearning. She missed home and the library, so she decided to go back.

Chapter Four: Secret Army

She returned to the library. She felt alive for the first time in her life, driven by a sense of purpose and passion that she had never experienced before. And so, Lily continued her journey through the library's halls, uncovering hidden fresh stories and adventures. One day, as she was browsing through an ancient book, Miss Adelaide came over and said: I need your help, Lily.

What do you need?" Lily asked, her curiosity piqued. Miss Adelaide took Lily to a secret room in the library, where a group of rebels were gathered. The room was full of people, some of whom she recognized from the library. They were sitting around a large table, which was covered in maps of the city and its surrounding areas. They were planning a revolution against the oppressive government that ruled their land. Lily listened intently as they discussed their plans."

The rebels explained to Lily that they wanted to overthrow the government and create a new, fairer system of rule. They asked Lily to join them in their cause and use her powers for good.Lily was hesitant at first, overwhelmed by the idea of taking on such a big responsibility. But then she thought of all the injustices that she had seen in her world and how much good she could do if given the chance.

Their plans strained like the lines and lines of a million words on a million sentences and she could picture the scenes unfolding in her mind: the meeting room would be cluttered with maps and strategy sheets, with pens and tables and a large, leather-bound book. The lamps in the room would be fully lit, giving the dark stains on the walls a looming, shifting, three-dimensional quality.

The secret room in the library was empty. Only candles and the rebels. She could see them talking and planning. Her heart swells with a newfound sense of purpose. She knew that this was an opportunity to make a real difference in the world. She feels the pain of the oppressed, and her heart swells with passion.

The power of the rebel group was growing, and soon news spread to the ears of the government. Acting quickly, they dispatched their soldiers to locate and put an end to this rebellion once and for all. When they arrived on the scene, Lily knew she had to act fast before any innocent lives were lost in a senseless battle and jumped into action!

Lily took a deep breath and stepped forward, her boots crunching on the gravel path as she approached the group of rebels. The wind picked up in a sudden gust, playing with her hair and pulling at the edges of her cloak. She could feel the eyes of the other fighters on her, watching and sizing her up. Determination etched into every line of her face as she joined the rebels to fight for justice. The weight of responsibility settled onto her shoulders like a heavy backpack, but Lily welcomed it with open arms, ready to make a difference. Her hands blazing with newfound magical power. She grabbed her newfound powers with both hands and tapped into what felt like an untapped energy source within herself, harnessing every ounce of strength that was inside her heart and jumped into action!

Her hands are ready, palms up, fingers curled. As she opens her palms, a ball of flame bursts into existence, a white-hot core the size of a tennis ball. Lily pushes her hands, fingers wide like an orchestra conductor, and the flame slowly expands into a burning sphere the size of a basketball.

She created a magical shield around them that rendered their foes unable to penetrate it, thus allowing them time to formulate an escape plan without being discovered or harmed in any way by those looking for them.

She sent illusions crashing into the government's soldiers, blinding them with a thousand lying visions. Her hands were blue with new power, and she sent the soldiers stumbling like blind men toppling off precarious ledges, their stiff backs turned to the sky. She sent dreams crashing down, and moonlight shining through their brains to destroy them in their dreams.

Meanwhile, Lily directed members from the rebels safely away from danger. Eventually, after hours elapsing under pressure, the rebels made a successful retreat back towards safety due largely thanks to her interventions! Everyone rejoiced but understood there are still more battles ahead if freedom is ever going to reach its full potential again over time. As Lily looked around at all the happy faces celebrating their victory, she knew that this was just the beginning, but what an incredible start it was! Lily's reputation as a fearless warrior grew, inspiring even more people to join the movement for change

As the revolution gained momentum, Lily found herself falling for one rebel, a dashing young man with bright blue eyes and a charming smile. Their love was fierce and passionate, but it was forbidden by society's strict rules. Lily's heart ached with the knowledge that their love was one that could never be fully accepted by the society. She knew about tragic ends for forbidden loves, and she did not want to suffer the same fate as other star-crossed lovers in history or even something like nobleman and the queen, although both of them had a good life but they never could be with each other for the rest of their life. She knew that the only way to make her love flourish was to win this revolution and take away the oppressive power of their government.

Lily and her beloved pledged themselves to the revolution, and together with their comrades, they forged ahead into battle. The wind picked up in a sudden gust, playing with her hair and pulling at the edges of her cloak. She could feel the eyes of the other fighters on her, watching and sizing her up. Lily stood tall, determination etched into every line of her face as she joined the rebels to fight for justice. The weight of responsibility settled onto her shoulders like a heavy backpack, but Lily welcomed it with open arms, ready to make a difference.

Whenever there was a battle her hands blazed with magical power. And ready, palms up, fingers curled. As she opens her palms, a ball of flame bursts into existence, a white-hot core the size of a tennis ball. Lily pushes her hands, fingers wide like an orchestra conductor, and the flame slowly expands into a burning sphere the size of a basketball.

The sound of a roaring campfire, the crackling of trees and wood being crushed beneath the feet of an army, a whirling wind stuck in a tornado, the rumble of falling hills and mountains, the crash of ocean waves against a rocky shoreline.

In many battles she sent illusions crashing into the government's soldiers, blinding them with a thousand lying visions. Her hands were infused with a potent new power, causing the soldiers to stumble like blind men toppling off treacherous ledges, she sent dreams crashing down, and moonlight shining through their brains to destroy them in their dreams.

With each and every step they took, Lily could almost feel her heart beating faster with anticipation. Finally, a chance to make a difference in this world and bring justice to those who have been oppressed for too long.

She and her love formed an unbreakable bond as they led their troops into battle. With every swing of their swords and every spell cast by Lily's powerful hands, they fought fiercely against their enemy.

When the dust settled after the victorious fight, Lily found herself to be alone on the battlefield. She felt a strange feeling inside her; she felt the presence of Miss Adelaide there, Miss Adelaide placed a hand on Lily's shoulder. "Don't worry, my dear. I know just what to do."

With that, Miss Adelaide began to chant a strange incantation, her hands glowing with a soft white light. And it was normal again she was in the circle of her comrades.

"What happened?" Lily asked?

Miss Adelaide explained to her when Lily threw herself into the fight, taking risks and pushing her abilities to their limits. Her connection to this world disconnected and after Jonathan died in the battle, she decided to be with him.

She turned to Lily and said: Love is a powerful force, but it can also be dangerous. You must be careful, Lily." The only reason that you are still here alive is because you knew that you would never give up fighting for what you believe in.

But I wanted to be with Jonathan, you should let me alone, I fight because I don't believe in the norms of society. I know you want to fight for your love and that is very brave of you and it is noble but you have a greater purpose than your love. Lily nodded; her heart weighed down with responsibility for her mission. She shouldn't think about herself alone.

Lily returned to the rebels' camp and continued to fight for their cause, her heart filled with both love and determination. Finally, after months of hard work and dedication, peace was restored in the nation. And while conflicts still remained between them, the government agreed to make several changes to the rules and give freedom to people.

Lily had done what many thought impossible; she had changed history forever; by following through with her dreams of achieving justice, which had enabled people all over the world to have access to freedoms that were previously just out of reach for so many years. Lily realized that the true magic of the library lay not in the hidden treasures, but in the stories themselves.

The library was a gateway to worlds unknown, a place where mysteries could be unraveled, and dreams could take flight. From that day forward, Lily became the guardian of the library's secrets, sharing its wonders with all who sought them. And as for the enchanted book, it remained a mystery, its blank pages a reminder that the greatest stories are the ones we create ourselves, with every turn of the page. Lily embraced her role as the guardian of the library's secrets with unwavering dedication. She spent countless hours meticulously organizing the shelves, ensuring that each book found its rightful place. "Seal of Solomon" book however, remained an enigma. Its blank pages held the promise of endless possibilities, urging Lily to embark on her own creative journey. Determined to unlock its secrets, she delved into the depths of her imagination, crafting stories that would captivate readers for generations to come. Lily understood that the true magic of storytelling lay not only in the words written on the pages but also in the stories we create ourselves, with every turn of the page.

Lily's dedication to the library's secrets extended beyond the organization of its shelves. She delved into the history of each book, uncovering hidden tales and forgotten narratives. Her research led her to discover the ancient art of book restoration, a skill she eagerly acquired to preserve the library's treasures. With delicate hands and a keen eye, Lily breathed new life into worn-out pages, allowing the stories within to be cherished by future generations. As she worked, she couldn't help but feel a deep sense of gratitude for the authors who had poured their hearts and souls into their creations. Through her efforts, the library became a sanctuary for knowledge and a hub of intellectual curiosity. Lily's dedication and love for the library's secrets had not only preserved its treasures but had also created a haven for the power of words to thrive. The library became a place where imaginations soared, where dreams were nurtured, and a world where their love would be accepted, where they could attest their love and not fear its consequences.

One day, as Lily sat in the library's gardens, lost in thought, she heard a voice behind her. "Did you miss me? "

Lily turned around to see who it was, it was Sam.

She saw him standing in the distance. Dressed in black, his face hidden by shadows.

When she saw Sam standing before her, her eyes filled with rage. All the memories of the dark moment rushed into her head. Lily smelled the putrid scent of death and decay all around her. The sun smells like burning hydrogen and metal. Her muscles tensed and quivered, with a soft fizzle of static radiating off her. The back of her throat grew dry and salty, as if she had swallowed a mouthful of the sea. Her mouth was filled with the taste of blood. It coated her tongue and coated her gums.

What do you want from me? Lily asked.

I want you, Lily. I can't stop thinking about you, Sam replied.

He brushed a strand of hair from Lily's face, his touch sending shivers down her spine. Then he reached out to grab her hand.

I want to protect you; you are in danger, Sam added.

How do you want to protect me? You belong to darkness, I never forget the last time I trusted you, Lily said angrily.

Sam's face fell at Lily's words, his eyes downcast. "I know I've made mistakes in the past, Lily. But I promise you, I've changed. I want to be someone you can trust, someone who can protect you from the dangers of this world."

Your burden is too much, let me help you and carry your weight, I can lift it from your shoulder, Sam added.

Sam squeezed her hand gently, his eyes meeting hers. "I understand your fears, Lily. But I promise you, I will do everything in my power to protect you. We can fight for a better future together."

Lily felt her resolve falter in the face of Sam's words. He had always been a control manipulator, but this time, his passion was obvious and undeniable. His earnestness was captivating, yet she wasn't sure if it was his own ambition or for their shared cause that drove him now. She wanted to believe him, but she wasn't sure if she could trust him.

She pulled her hand away from his grasp. "I need time to think, Sam. I can't just forget about everything that's happened between us. "Sam nodded, his expression solemn. "I understand. Take all the time you need, Lily. But know that I will always be here for you, no matter what."

Lily watched as Sam disappeared into the shadows, his figure fading into the darkness. She struggled to choose between her mission and the fear of his betrayal. She knew that she needed to be careful, trust her instincts and not let her heart rule her head. Also, she wanted to find out the truth about her grandfather.

As she walked back into the library, she couldn't help but feel grateful for the sanctuary it provided. It was a place where she could lose herself in the magic of books, where the stories within its walls offered a respite from the chaos of the outside world. She needed allies she could trust, people who understood the power of words and the importance of keeping them safe. Miss Adelaide had gone for a while, and she wasn't around to help her, and her lover also was not around to help.

Lily walked through the library's halls, her mind racing with thoughts of what she needed to do next. As she turned a corner, she saw a figure standing at the end of the hallway. It was an old man, his face weathered and lined with age. With a book clasped in his hands, his attention was solely devoted to the pages before him.

Lily approached him, her curiosity piqued. "Excuse me, sir. Can I help you with something?" The old man looked up at her, his eyes meeting hers. "Ah, Lily. I've been hoping to run into you." Lily furrowed her brow, her mind racing with questions. "Do I know you?"

The old man chuckled, his eyes twinkling with amusement. "Not yet my dear. But I believe we share a common interest."

Lily's curiosity grew stronger. "What interest is that?"

"Books, my dear. The stories they hold, the secrets they keep, the power they possess. I have spent my entire life studying them, cherishing them, preserving them. And now, I believe it's time for me to pass on my knowledge to someone who shares my passion."

The old man smiled, her eyes shining with a fierce intensity. I can answer your questions about the past, especially about Arthur. You have learned about the magic world and secrets of the library, now it is the time that you learn about Arthur and what happened to him.

Lily felt a flicker of recognition, the old man's words striking a chord within her. "How do you know what happened to him? Old man smiled warmly, his eyes crinkling at the corners. "I've been watching you, Lily. Watching as you pour your heart and soul into this library.

Lily felt she could trust him and said: I have learned a lot during past years, I never knew magic exists and now I can do magic. First time I walked into this library; it was so strange. The first thing I saw was the ambiance, the place was beautiful. The walls, the floor and the bookshelves, all painted in different shades of different colors, it was like being inside a human heart.

The second thing I noticed was the smell. It was so strong and spicy and unexplainable. The smell of knowledge, of history, of the past. The scent was barely perceptible as I entered: a subtle blend of oak, pipe, tobacco, and leather.

An odd mixture of ancient parchment and new leather-bound editions filled the air, delicious scents of words and knowledge. Heartache and loss, regret and hope, passion and love, despair and betrayal, life and death, romance and tragedy, desire and obsession, sorrow and tears, longing and love, hate and fear.

The third thing I felt was the touch of the books. Not the books, the covers. They were so smooth and soft, as if they were made with love. The door's surface greeted my fingertips with a cool and soothing sensation. When I turned the knob, the wood felt smooth against the back of my hand.

The library's stone pillars and oak door handles felt rough and ancient, but the leather-bound books in front of me were smooth as glass. They seemed to whisper to me, enticing me to touch them. And then "seal of Solomon" with invisible ink.

Stop right there, an old man interrupted her.

Lily was taken aback by his sudden interruption. "What is it?" she asked, her curiosity piqued once more. The old man's expression grew grave, his eyes narrowed. "The Seal of Solomon, you say? That is a dangerous and powerful artifact, one that should not be taken lightly."

Lily's heart quickened at the man's words. "Why is it dangerous?"

The old man sighed, his expression growing distant. "The Seal of Solomon is not the one that you think, those who seek to possess it must be careful, lest they unleash forces they cannot control." You may think the only forbidden thing in the book is forbidden love, but that book holds lots of secrets which are forbidden. You may even awaken dark spirits or the devil himself.

Lily felt a chill run through her spine, the weight of the man's words settling heavily on her shoulders. "What should I do?" she asked, her voice barely above a whisper.

The old man fixed on her with a serious look. "You must be careful, Lily. The Seal of Solomon is not something to be trifled with. You must study it carefully and only use its power for good. Otherwise, you risk unleashing darkness upon the world."

Lily nodded, her determination growing stronger. "I understand. I will be careful and study it thoroughly. Thank you for warning me."

The old man smiled, a glimmer of pride in his eyes. "I knew you were special the moment I saw you, Lily. You have the power to change the world with your words and your passion. Never forget that."

I can help you achieve great things. Old man said.

Lily stood there momentarily, immersed in contemplation. You must give me permission to help you, give me your hand, Lily hesitated, but then slowly stretched out her hand. She felt a strange warmth course through him as the old man grabbed it in both of hers and began to chant softly in a strange language, almost like he was praying or casting some kind of spell.

The room grew colder and darker as the chanting continued until finally Lily felt something brush against her soul, seemingly from all directions at once. It was almost euphoric, yet terrifying at the same time; she shivered slightly despite feeling more grounded than ever before, like she could take on anything that comes along with newfound strength and courage inside herself. When the chanting stopped, silence filled its wake, only broken by the old man's soft words. "You are now under my protection, Lily. "And he disappeared.

She thought, what about Artur, he didn't tell me anything about Arthur? "You are under my protection "what does it mean?

She went to the library to look for the "seal of Solomon." It's said that the seal holds the key to unlocking the secrets of the universe, but at a substantial cost. Those who seek its power risk losing their souls to the darkness."

The Seal of Solomon held such immense power yet carried with it such great danger. She knew that she had to be careful if she wanted to uncover its secrets and keep the library safe.

But her thoughts kept drifting back to Arthur. The old man had promised her answers, yet she still knew nothing of his fate. She decided to delve deeper into the library's archives, hoping to uncover something that could shed light on the mystery.

After hours of searching, Lily stumbled upon an old letter tucked away in a forgotten corner of the library. It was addressed to Miss Adelaide, dated many years ago. As she read through the letter, she could feel her heart racing with a mixture of excitement and fear.

The letter revealed that Arthur had been working on a secret project, one that involved the Seal of Solomon. It had disappeared under mysterious circumstances, leaving behind only a cryptic message about the "key to unlocking the past."

She couldn't get access to Miss Adelaide to ask her about the letter, so she decided to reveal the coded message in the letter; she had done it before, when she first found "seal of the Solomon" with invisible ink.

She knew that she had to be careful if she wanted to uncover its secret. She went to find "seal of Solomon" in the special section of the library, because the letter was talking about the book. When she found it and grabbed the book, Lily's heart pounded, almost as if it were trying to break out of her ribcage and run away.

Lily's heart pounds in a violent rhythm, punctuated by the rhythm of her breathing. The Seal of Solomon was glowing a hazy yellow, as if the sun had been condensed into a tiny sphere in its center.

The Seal of Solomon was not to be taken lightly. But she couldn't shake the feeling that there was more to the story than what she was being told. She had to know the truth, no matter the cost.

A thumping noise like the echo of a war drum began to pierce through the library walls. Lily's heart pounds as she hears the sharp cry of a bird, and the distant sound of footsteps echoing through the library.

It was as loud as the bongo drums of the gods, the kind that could move mountains. With trembling hands, Lily opened the book. She was surprised because this time she could read the pages and it was not blank. As she read, the words on the page began to come alive. Maybe because she had unlocked the secret of the book before, but this time she was looking for something different, something that could lead her to Arthur and the encoded letter. She saw a phrase in the book, and she read it aloud: "revive the story of the man who unlocks the secret of this book for the first time."

The light bulbs above her faltered and flickered, casting a strobe effect across the room. The air grew thick with tension as she struggled to catch her breath in the pulsing lights. As the last bulb sputtered out, plunging everything into darkness, she felt something brush against her ankle and it sent shivers up her spine.

She remembered what happened last time, and she panicked, quickly she closed the book, but it was too late, darkness already was released, and it was getting physical shape. In the dark, she could see minor points of light. They were like fireflies. She could hear their noise like a swarm of bees getting closer and closer, and she could smell a stench of death, paint and decay. The hair on the back of her neck stood up, the scent was that of death and it was getting stronger. Her hands and arms were tingling as if asleep, and when she willed them to move, nothing happened. It was as if they had been paralyzed by a magic spell.

Lily could make out the vague outline of a person dancing in front of her, its eyes were like blue flames and its feet moved so fast they looked like they were on fire.

She smelled a sweet metallic smell like blood. Lily raised a hand to her nose and sniffed it. She smelled something like burning birch bark and burning leaves. She could hear the snap and pop of branches burning under the heat of the sun.

The thing kept growing and growing, its voice was like a loud whisper, it was slow and deliberate. It seemed as if it were talking to her. "You are under my protection now."

At this moment she realized she had made a mistake again and she shouldn't have trusted that man.

Her skin felt icy cold, like she had dipped her hand into a lake, and it had frozen over. It was cold and wet, as if she had walked in a puddle of water. The touch was clammy and creepy. The skin crawled up her leg, leaving an icy trail of slime. It was like a snake slithering up your leg. It slithered up her body, wrapping itself around her waist and squeezing her. At first, she thought it was snakes, but it didn't feel like skin.

She was suffocating and again Miss Adelaide came to rescue her.

You can fight it Lily, Miss Adelaide said.

She grabbed the book, opened it, and read a sentence from the page. Revive the story of the first woman in the book. Lily felt a sudden burst of energy and grip of the forces of darkness get loose, but she was still under her protection as a Veil of darkness. She watched the man's eyes become solid black, and the pupil vanished. Her irises were like black holes that led into an eternal abyss.

She saw something inside the book, a Veil of darkness. She saw it move toward her, trying to take control. She heard screaming, and she heard something like a loud roar, like a hungry animal. The man's voice was as loud as thunder.

The sound of screams echoed in her mind, skin being ripped from flesh, bones being cracked, blood-curdling cries, drowning in agony, the silence after the torture. As the darkness that had taken over her body.

Her skin felt like it was electrified, like she had put her hand on a power line, but at the same time it felt like it was being ripped off by the force. Her skin felt like it was electrified, like putting your hand on a power line. The touch of the man was cold, like the touch of death. She felt the pain, the grief, the death and decay, the sadness, the loss of self and the depression that comes with it. She felt as if she was suffocating.

Miss Adelaide continuously encouraged her to fight. She slowly stood up and faced the creature with new courage. She recites from the book again; she was born in darkness, but out of darkness, she found her way into light. She conquered fear with her courage and stood up against injustice. She was strong-willed, determined, and brave, and she showed us that anything is possible."

As Lily finished reciting the words, a bright light shone around them both. The creature in front of her seemed to shrink away in fear as it realized it could not overpower Lily anymore. The dark veil surrounding them slowly disappeared until only a faint glimmer was left in its place.

Lily looked at the creature one last time before turning away, knowing that whatever evil power it possessed could no longer harm her or anyone else anymore. Taking a deep breath, Lily walked away with her head held high. With each step towards freedom, she felt lighter and more empowered than ever before.

The sweet smell of roses filled her nostrils and grew more intense with every passing second. It was so strong that it made her head spin. She felt a sense of warmth and comfort come over her body as the rose petals caressed her skin like gentle waves.

She opened the book and began to read the words on the page. As she read, it was as if she was transported to another world, with the story of the first woman written in its pages. She could feel herself being brought back to life by these ancient words.

She heard a voice whisper in her ear, "You will always be safe. Spinning around, she saw Miss Adelaide standing there smiling at her, then fading away into nothing but a memory. As Lily stood in awe of what had just happened, she looked down to see the book clasped tightly in her hands. Taking one last look at it before putting it back on the shelf, she thought about how much this book meant to her and all that it had brought out of her during such a chaotic time.

Lights got back to the room and everything became normal. The sweetness of roses grew stronger as the smell grew more intense. Lily hasn't found anything about Arthur's destiny yet, but she was afraid to open the book and read it again.It was dark outside; she decided to go back home to her grandfather.

Chapter Five: Back in Time

It was dinner time when Lily opened the door of the house, her grandfather was setting the table.

You come at the right time, Arthur said.

I am so hungry, Lily responds.

Can you grab my medication from my pocket, Arthur asked?

Yes, sure I will get it to you right away, Lily answered.

When Lily went upstairs to get the medication she found an old letter in the pocket of her grandfather's coat, which turns out to be a coded message. Lily put it back but determined to unravel the mystery that her grandfather had.

When they were having dinner Lily asked: you never talked about the first time you came to this town.

Oh, it is nothing, it will be boring for you, Arthur said.

But I like to hear your story, Lily insisted.

Ok, when I was new to town, I went to the library and found lots of interesting books about different places. Because I love to travel, I used those books to travel to those places. If you are interested, I can give you my logbook, I recorded everything on it.

Lily was so excited, she spent many hours poring over the logbook, studying each page intently. It had been many years since this book had been written, but it revealed some interesting information about Miss Adelaide.

The logbook detailed her grandfather's travels, and his relationship with a woman named Madeline. The logbook also contained coded messages that Lily struggled to decipher. Finally, Lily found a letter from many years ago with Madeline's name on it.

In that letter her grandfather asked Madeline to help her get back his magic power.

Lily was determined to finish the mission her grandfather had started so many years ago, but she knew it would be difficult.

The truth was that Miss Adelaide had been searching for a lost book that her grandfather (Arthur) had taken from the library many years ago. The book was called 'The Seal of Solomon', and it was said to contain powerful magic. Legend has it that anyone who possessed this book will have the power to control all living things, however they wished. When she found the book for the first time, she could decipher the coded message inside the book and she knew what kind of book it is.

Lily knew how powerful it is, not only powerful, but also dangerous. Her grandfather had found the book, unlocked the secret and got its magic but had lost its power due to using it for his own benefit. Lily remembered traveling to another dimension with her grandfather and she was thinking is it possible that her grandfather regains his magical power. She has the book of "seal of Solomon", and she has the power of magic, maybe she could help her grandfather regain his power as well. Fortunately, Lily's grandfather had left her some clues about how to do that. In his logbook, he wrote about mysterious symbols he saw in an old temple near the library. He believed these symbols could connect the library to his hometown, but he never managed to solve them while he got his power.

She entered her grandfather's room with a heavy heart, determined to share her decision. But instead of listening quietly, the old man flew into a rage. "No! You must not do this, it is too perilous," he shouted, his voice rough and strained with emotion. "I am too old now; I cannot protect you. Leave the book and job to Miss Adelaide!" Tears shone in his eyes as he finished his sentence, an edge of aggression still lacing his words.

But why? I want to know why you lost the magical power; I remember we used to go to another dimension together; you showed me so many places, why did you leave me in the dark Lily asked?

Stop it, you don't understand, go fetch Miss Adelaide, I want to talk to her, grandfather said firmly.

She left the room wondering what happened to her grandfather. He was not himself that day.

She was shocked by her grandfather's reaction, but she was determined to solve the problem. A few days later, Miss Adelaide came from the trip. Lily explained to her what had happened and what was her grandfather's reaction.

Miss Adelaide finally conceded that she had been a substitute for her grandfather, as it would mean he couldn't regain his lost power. She explained to Lily that during a journey into the realm of spirits, her grandfather tried out some forbidden magic to try to regain his strength. Unfortunately, it had worked against him and instead of restoring his power; he was banned from the library. He cannot enter the library due to magical power he previously possessed.

Lily's heart sank with saddened understanding of Miss Adelaide's words, but she was determined not to give up even if restoring grandfather's magical powers wasn't part of it. After much thought and discussion among them both, Lily realized the only way she can help her grandfather is to take on her grandfather's role in order to bring balance back. By taking over, she will be able to continue what grandfather started many years ago in a search for magic of "The Seal of Solomon."

One day while she was going through books in the library, she discovered a secret about magical power. If she could get back in time, she could influence the events, although with doing that her future may be changed too.

She decided to do that, but she needed to master another skill, travel through time. She had learned a lot of things before, and she can learn this skill too.

Lily began studying every book she could find on time travel. It was a difficult and dangerous skill to master, but she knew it was the only way to save her grandfather's powers.

She spent months locked away in the library day after day, practicing and honing her skills until finally, with a burst of energy and determination, Lily disappeared into thin air.

When she opened her eyes again, everything had changed. She stood in front of an ancient building, before entering, Lily found herself surrounded by heavily armed guards demanding how have you come here?

"This place is forbidden for non-royal members."

She said she is coming from another time and another kingdom.

They took a moment discussing allowing someone from another

kingdom inside such an important place. With great effort & tactful convincing behavior, Lilly managed to get past them without much resistance.

Upon stepping into the premises, she encountered numerous chambers brimming with knowledge surpassing one's wildest imagination, finding something that could help her would take some time.Lily didn't know what she was looking for exactly, she was looking for signs to help her find a clue. After weeks of traveling through corridors and doorways that led nowhere near it became clear that someone was trying to stop her from discovering its location, someone who knew exactly what kind of power could be unleashed if it fell into certain hands. It was like a maze; you could get lost in the temple easily. One day while traveling through medieval times, Lily came across a room, it had a giant door. Inside was a small open wooden box on the floor, and the room smelled like a chemical lab.

She stumbled upon an old man wearing all white sitting on a wooden box. His eyes glow white. His hair is jet black. His skin is pale.

Who are you? asked Lily, rather surprised.

'I am Merlin', He said calmly. When the old man speaks, you could taste the magic on his breath and you could taste the magic deep inside you.the smell of roasting meat and burnt wood filled her nose, as the smell of the candles came to her.

Lily recognized his name immediately, "the most powerful wizard" she thought.

Merlin looked at Lilly more closely. His eyes sparkled when he saw something special in this young woman "You must have come here seeking magical knowledge.

Merlin asked.

I am looking for a way to restore my grandfather's magic power, Lily said.

"Hummmm", how so, why did your grandfather lose his power?

He made a mistake, but if I find the actual "seal of Solomon", I can restore his magical power, Lily prompted.

Merlin stroked his beard, deep in thought. "Finding the Seal of Solomon will not be a simple task," he said finally. "It is protected by powerful magic and guarded by creatures beyond your wildest imagination."

"I am willing to do whatever it takes, "Lily replied determinedly.

Merlin nodded solemnly at her response. "Very well then, I shall help you on your quest. "He stood up from the wooden box and began pacing back and forth in front of her.

"The first step is to obtain a magical key that unlocks the entrance to where The Seal lies hidden," Merlin explained. "But alas, this key has been missing for years."

"Do you know anything about its whereabouts? "Asked Lily with hopeful eyes.

"Yes, but..." Merlin hesitated before continuing slowly: "To get hold of this mysterious key, we need something that belongs solely only for King Arthur."

Lily's eyes widened. "King Arthur?" she repeated in disbelief. "But I thought he was just a legend."

Merlin chuckled at her reaction. "Oh, my dear Lily," he said with a twinkle in his eye, "sometimes legends are more than just stories." He paused for effect before continuing.

"King Arthur did excitant some of his belongings have been passed down to the next generation by those who knew him best. One such item is the Sword of Excalibur."

Lily shook her head with unbelief. She had always heard about King Arthur and Excalibur growing up, but to think that they might actually play a role in her quest seemed too incredible to be true.

"How can we find this sword? "She asked Merlin eagerly.

"It won't be easy," replied Merlin firmly. "The Sword of Excalibur has its own powerful magic, only someone pure hearted enough can wield it without being consumed by its power."

"I am willing to try anything."

"Very well then, "said Merlin with an approving nod." We shall set out on our journey tomorrow morning at dawn." With that, he began muttering incantations under his breath as candle flames flickered around them both…

The next morning, Lily and Merlin set out on their journey to find Excalibur. They rode horses through thick forests, over babbling brooks, and across vast meadows as they searched for any sign of the sword's whereabouts.

As they approached a small village nestled in between two mountains, Merlin pointed towards the largest mountain. "There, "he said with certainty. "I can feel its presence."

Lily squinted her eyes in amazement at how anyone could sense an item from so far away. "Let's hurry then," she urged him on as they spurred their horses onwards up into the rugged terrain where few had ever dared venture before.

After several hours of burdensome climbing under blistering sun rays which left them panting profusely like dogs upon reaching wherever poised within sight, Merlin suddenly stopped by a cave entrance concealed behind boulder cracks looming ahead amidst jagged rocks jutting out precariously everywhere nearby around it gloomy shrouded by descending clouds overhead while Lily scanned surrounding areas warily for signs danger lurking anywhere else hidden.

"We must be cautious here," warned Merlin as gravely gestured for me to follow him. I couldn't help but feel a sense of unease. I knew that whatever lay beyond that ominous opening would be trouble, yet here I was, following him. My mind raced with thoughts of danger and uncertainty. Why did he drag me into this? What awaited us inside? I stayed close behind him, wary of any sudden movements or unexpected surprises lurking in the shadows. Gravely seemed uneasy too, his steps hesitant as he led the way. We were both on edge, and for good reason. Whatever we found inside could change everything. I had no choice but to continue forward.

Lily's heart was racing with anticipation, and fear as she followed Merlin into the dark cave. The air grew colder, and their footsteps echoed against the walls of stone, suddenly, there was a glint of light ahead. As they drew closer, Lily could see that it was Excalibur in all its glory, lying upon a pedestal made of solid gold.

Merlin held up his hand and whispered an incantation to ward off any potential dangers lurking within the caverns.as he approached

Excalibur slowly, he sensed a cloaked over weapon by someone powerful enough to try concealing it from view, those without the purest hearts able withstand its power grip hilt properly. Merlin said: you can grab it now.

Lily's hand hovered in the air, trembling, as her lips moved in silent prayer. She hesitated before gathering her courage and finally reaching for the handle, bracing herself for whatever might come but suddenly something unexpected happened, an invisible force pushed her away from the sword! And at that same moment, they both heard loud evil laughter coming seemingly from every direction around them!

"Be careful! "Warned Merlin urgently as he stood back up after being knocked down harshly indeed.

"What is this Sorcery?" cried out Lilly perplexedly, unable to control her fear any longer.

Merlin frantically searched the surrounding area with his wand, trying to locate the source of the evil sorcery that was attacking them.

Suddenly, amidst all this confusion and chaos, a dark figure emerged from behind Excalibur. The stranger was tall and muscular, adorned in a hooded robe that concealed his features entirely but for glowing red eyes shining intensely within darkness where face should have been seen instead; it seemed as if they were looking into pure fire itself, which burned with demonic hunger, born out abyssal flames unknown till now!

"Who are you?" demanded Merlin boldly, while drawing upon magical reserves within to combat this menace, supposedly confronting them outright.

The stranger chuckled softly before replying in mocking tone, "You shall address me as your king, for I am Morgathor ruler of these caverns! And whoever wishes to possess mighty Excalibur will have faced my wrath!"

Merlin stood firm despite seemingly overwhelming odds against him whilst casting enchanted spells towards Morgathor With hope in his heart, the brave warrior hoped to subdue him long enough to retrieve the priceless artifact that was needed to save the magic If not, they would surely suffer nightmarish horrors unendurable.

But Morgathor was not so easily subdued. He laughed maniacally as he deflected Merlin's spells effortlessly with a flick of his wrist. "Foolish wizard, your puny magic is no match for me, and Excalibur will be mine!" he bellowed. Lilly stood frozen in fright, but her fear soon turned to anger at the sight of this evil creature trying to steal the legendary sword that rightfully belonged to King Arthur and his descendants. She knew she had to act fast before it was too late.

With all her might, Lilly threw fire towards Morgathor hoping to catch him off guard and knock him down so they could retrieve Excalibur from behind him. But as soon as she tried that, he swiftly turned around and hit Lilly on the face with the back of his hand, causing her to collide with a wall close by. Merlin screamed in fury upon seeing what happened, but still held steadfast against immeasurable sorcery unleashed without caring cost himself or anyone else involved.

Morgathor moved closer towards them, holding deadly intent written on every inch of body, definitely ready to slaughter any who dared resist pointlessly versus inevitable fate awaiting here now; hence forcing them back step by step until there was nowhere left to go anymore trapped like cornered animals facing hunters.

But just when all hope seemed lost, a deep rumbling sound filled the cavern, causing Morgathor to pause momentarily. The ground was shaking, and Merlin could feel something powerful approaching. Suddenly, a massive dragon burst through the ceiling of the cave and landed between them and Morgathor.

Morgathor snarled with rage at this new challenger, but it was clear that he had met his match against this giant beast. With one swift movement of its tail, the dragon sent Morgathor flying across the cave, where he hit his head on a stalagmite before falling unconscious to the ground.

Merlin and Lilly couldn't believe their luck as they looked upon this magnificent creature who had saved them from certain doom. The dragon advanced towards them, its golden eyes piercing through the darkness of the cave. Its rainbow colored scales shimmered in a mesmerizing blue-green hue, something that none of them would ever forget in the hours to follow. Attempting to describe such an unearthly beauty seemed futile, no words could sum up all that they saw before them. In comparison to its grandeur, their own insignificance was painfully apparent as they pondered upon the mystery of human existence and searched for purpose in this vast nothingness with eventual death as only absolute certainty.

"Who are you?" whispered Lilly softly, afraid she might startle it away.

The dragon regarded her for a moment before answering in a deep, rumbling voice that seemed to shake the cave itself. "I am Valtari, the protector of these lands," it said.

Merlin stepped forward and bowed respectfully. "Thank you for saving us, "he said with admiration evident in his voice.

Valtari dipped its head graciously. "It was my pleasure to come to your aid," it replied before turning back towards Lilly, who had taken an involuntary step backwards at Merlin's gesture of respect toward this colossal creature.

"Do not be afraid, little one,"

Valtari spoke softly, understanding the immense fear this towering beast provoked in her. She felt cowering beneath it, like a sheep surrounded by herd hunters, waiting outside the barrier that separated them. There was nothing standing between their fates besides their quick wits and nimble feet, as well as any lucky strikes or timely interventions they could make. The same sorts of interactions had just been witnessed moments ago, yet still lingered just beyond her peripheral vision, unsettling every nerve raw from the adrenaline pumping through her veins. She could barely keep her composure under the menacing presence looming above her in the hierarchy that had already been established. She thought submission would be required without question and knew that it was time to find a way to escape. Yet there seemed to be no hope of regaining freedom if she returned.

"I do not wish you harm," Valtari continued, my mission is to protect this land and its people from a rising evil that threatens us all."

Lilly listened intently; her fear momentarily forgotten as Valtari spoke of a great danger facing their land. Merlin stepped forward once more and nodded his understanding.

Why do you need this sword? Dragon asked.

We need it to get hold of the key for unlocking the past, Lily responds.

You need to embark on a journey over tall mountains, beyond the reach of ordinary people, into a valley shrouded in morning mist. There, you will discover a sacred place that is only known to those with pure hearts and a willingness to encounter challenges that the human mind cannot grasp. To accomplish this task, you must complete seemingly impossible missions in order to obtain a precious artifact. This artifact is desired by many, but only a few have ever had the honor of holding it, even if just for a moment, amidst their struggles. In order to succeed, you must listen to the wise whispers of the sages, who will guide you on your path and prevent you from succumbing to the weaknesses and distractions that may tempt you and alter your future forever.

Merlin's eyes widened at the mention of such potent magic.

"Where would we begin our search? "He asked eagerly.

Valtari gestured with one massive, clawed foot towards the entrance of the cave, where warm sunlight filtered through cracks in stone walls draped resplendently by smooth red velvet pouring down waterfalls like liquid fire.

Lilly felt a shiver run down her spine as she looked at the entrance of the cave, unsure if they would even make it out alive. But Merlin seemed resolute and determined, his eyes sparkling with excitement and curiosity.

"We shall begin our journey there," he declared boldly.

And so began their quest to retrieve the precious artifact that could unlock the secrets of their past. They traveled across mountains high beyond realm mortals into valley hidden misty dawn, facing challenges the mortal mind couldn't comprehend. They fought off dangerous beasts lurking in every corner, overcame impossible tasks requiring great strength and resilience.

Each time they thought their journey was done; a new trial awaited them. But with Valtari's guidance and Merlin's courage, nothing seemed impossible for them to tackle. Finally, after many months on the trail of adventure and danger, they succeeded in retrieving the key from its hidden place, guarded by celestial powers beyond imagination.

With that magical key at last in their possession, Lilly stepped forward with trembling hands, ready to unlock what had been lost so long ago.she couldn't let herself be distracted from finding the artifact that would save her grandfather magic.The relic was said to contain immense power; Lilly could only begin to imagine what kind of forces were at play here. But with Merlin by her side, she felt stronger than ever before.

We have to go toward the enchanted library, Merlin said.

Ok, let's go back to the library, Lily responded.

No, not your library in the town, Merlin protested.

So, what library then, Lily abrupt.

As I was saying, there is an enchanted Library in Camelot where we found the Excalibur. Merlin added.

When they reached the library, there was a big door without any keyhole or any handle or knob.

Are you sure we came to the right place? Lily questioned.

I am sure, don't worry. Merlin confirmed.

What now? Lily Cross Examined.

Just tap the key to the door three times, Merlin responded.

When Lily tapped the door with the key three times, Door opened wide open. Together they poured through books on ancient myths and legends, searching for any mention of the lost artifact they sought. Days turned into weeks as they combed every inch of knowledge housed within these walls until finally something caught their eyes, a map detailing hidden passages leading directly towards location rumored to hold magical sources capable of destroying existence depending upon who wields it.

Lilly felt a wave of emotions as the realization hit her like a mountain, Lily's eyes began to well up with tears as realization struck this very treasure may have been what ruined her beloved granddad so long ago. She had blocked out the memory, knowing that it was to shield herself from true responsibility: carrying the weight of the legacy she had been given by birthright. She was destined to follow it no matter the cost, whether it be sacrificing herself or her soul, or even dying if necessary to protect the innocent and stay on the right cause's worth fighting for. Noble goals for noble needs, with a purpose that would light a fire at its blazing core that would burn brightly today, tomorrow and for eternity thereafter. It was this passion that drove her forward, consuming all the light in its darkest nights and fuelling her on.

Lilly and Merlin gazed at the map, tracing their fingers over each winding path and hidden entrance. This was it, the final clue to unlocking the location of the artifact they so desperately needed.

Excitement swelled within Lilly's chest as she realized that this would be her chance to honor her grandfather's legacy. She knew what had to be done, even if it meant sacrificing everything she held dear.

Without hesitation, Lilly set out on foot towards their destination with nothing but a backpack filled with supplies and determination in her heart – ready for whatever lay ahead.

As they journeyed deeper into unknown territory marked by rocky lush greenery all around them growth surrounded every step leading closer razor edge fate sacrifice called forth taking up mantle responsibility passed down from generation girl courageous enough stand firm ground face adversity danger overcome fears doubts find true self channel inner strength keep growing stronger day deserve title heroine onwards marks start true adventure slaying dragons saving kingdoms protecting weak strong alike rise against tyranny darkness reign supreme until balance restored peace prevails once more rightful beautiful land saved future secured past remembered always never forgotten millennia come gone time forgets good deeds live forevermore hearts souls people touched lives changed betterment humanity sake hope dreams inspiration carry torch flame lit bright shining example others emulate follow footsteps lead tomorrow brighter dawn breaking horizon heralding new era filled possibilities.

As she trekked through the rugged terrain, Lilly couldn't shake off the feeling of being watched. She turned around to see Merlin casting a weary glance at her. "Are you okay?" he asked.

Lily nodded, but deep down inside, she wasn't sure if she was ready for what lay ahead. The closer they got to their destination, the more dangerous things became - with perilous ravines and deadly creatures lurking around every corner.

But as they pushed forward towards their goal, nothing could stand in their way now that they had each other's backs. They crossed rivers teeming with crocodiles and scaled sheer cliffs holding on tight while fighting exhaustion coursing through veins, determination refusing to quit, never giving up resolve unwavering.

Finally, after days of travel so arduous it felt like eternity standing before them entrance leading underground catacombs shrouded mystery enigma cryptic markings adorning walls pillars illuminated candlelight glowing orbs strange crystals emanating pulsing energy yet again eerie sensation engulfed girl fierce bravery faced uncertainties life death beyond mere mortal comprehension.

Taking a deep breath, Lilly plunged headfirst into unknown depths following twisting turns of winding maze until finally arriving upon a chamber adorned with ancient artifacts signs symbols glyphs etched surface pottery drawings telling tales lost civilizations grandeur faded long ago leaving only whispers forgotten lore amidst musty air.

As she trekked through the rugged terrain, Lilly couldn't shake off the feeling of being watched. She turned around to see Merlin casting a weary glance at her. "Are you okay?" he asked.

Lily nodded, but deep down inside, she wasn't sure if she was ready for what lay ahead. The closer they got to their destination, the more dangerous things became - with perilous ravines and deadly creatures lurking around every corner.

As Lilly surveyed the chamber, she felt a sense of awe and

reverence. She had always been fascinated with history and here was an opportunity to witness it up close.

Merlin approached her, a grave expression on his face. "Lilly," he whispered, "this is where we part ways."

"What do you mean?" Lilly asked in confusion.

"I cannot accompany you any further," Merlin explained. "This journey ahead is meant for one person alone - the chosen one."

"But I'm not the chosen one!" protested Lilly.

"You are courageous enough to have come this far," said Merlin firmly. "And that's all that matters." With those words, he turned around and left without another word.

Feeling lost without her mentor at her side, Lily hesitated before taking another step forward – but then remembered why she came: To continue down this treacherous path in order to find what lay at its end.

Taking a deep breath; summoning courage from depths unknown plunging into darkness abyss light guiding way towards destiny bearing upon shoulders mantle responsibility greater than self-marked heroism imprinted soil time eternal courage unyielding adventuring deeper.

Flickering candlelight offered glimpses, fleeting shadows slithered across walls, whispers filled air, murmurs indiscernible voices in ancient languages long since lost memory bouncing off pillars.

Lilly continued to descend deeper into the catacombs, not letting fear take hold of her. She was determined to reach the end of this journey and uncover whatever secrets lay hidden in these chambers.as she walked further along, Lilly stumbled upon a strange tunnel leading off to one side. It looked ancient and unused compared to the larger tunnels she had been traveling through so far.

Curiosity getting the better of her, Lily decided against following Merlin's warning and ventured down that path. The air grew colder as she moved forward until reaching a small opening illuminated by an eerie purple glow emanating from behind it.

Finally, after days of travel so arduous it felt like eternity standing before them entrance leading underground catacombs shrouded mystery enigma cryptic markings adorning walls pillars illuminated candlelight glowing orbs strange crystals emanating pulsing energy yet again eerie sensation engulfed girl fierce bravery faced uncertainties life death beyond mere mortal comprehension.

Chapter Six: Seven Chamber

After all experience and after many sleepless nights and the exhaustion of all her troubleshooting efforts, she finally finds the relic that could solve the problem. When she returned, Lilly sat in the library and thought about her recent journey. She had faced so many challenges and obstacles, Valtari's warning echoed in her mind:

"Let us not succumb to temptation and distractions that come our way so that we may stay on the path that will determine our destiny."

She saw granddad in her mind's eye. His smile as she entered his room. The way he looked at her when she told him about the stories, he used to tell her when she was just a little girl. The time he took her out for ice cream. The way he would laugh when she made her silly mistakes.

She understood her granddad's situation was too far gone for her to fix; some mistakes were just too big to undo, and some mistakes are so big that you can't not correct them.

She also remembered Merlin who said "You are courageous enough to have come this far, "And that's all that matters."

Feeling lost without her mentor at her side, Lily hesitated before taking another step forward – but then remembered why she came: To continue down this treacherous path in order to find what lay at its end.

Taking a deep breath; summoning courage from depths unknown plunging into darkness abyss light guiding way towards destiny bearing upon shoulders mantle responsibility greater than self-marked heroism imprinted soil time eternal courage unyielding adventuring deeper.

Flickering candlelight offered glimpses, fleeting shadows slithered across walls, whispers filled air, murmurs indiscernible voices in ancient languages long since lost memory bouncing off pillars.

Lilly continued to descend deeper into the catacombs, not letting fear take hold of her. She was determined to reach the end of this journey and uncover whatever secrets lay hidden in these chambers.

As she walked further along, Lilly stumbled upon a strange tunnel leading off to one side. It looked ancient and unused compared to the larger tunnels she had been traveling through so far.

Curiosity getting the better of her, Lily decided to follow that path against Merlin's warning and ventured down that path. The air grew colder as she moved forward until finally reaching a small opening illuminated by an eerie purple glow emanating from behind it.

Cautiously she peered through the opening only to find a large room filled with mystical artifacts and mysterious symbols on every surface. She realized that this must be where her journey ends, for here lies the entrance to a series of trials designed for those brave enough to take them. a low rumbling voice sounded out in an unknown tongue: "You seek the truth but must first prove yourself worthy. You shall face seven trials before you." With that, several doorways appeared around her, each made of heavy stones engraved with ancient symbols and inscriptions unlike anything she had ever seen before.

Lilly gulped; overwhelmed by what lay ahead but determined to stay true on this journey and fulfill whatever tests were presented to her. She closed her eyes for a moment, summoning courage within, then opened them again and strode forward towards the first doorway ready for whatever may come next.

One trial after another she faced and overcame. Through danger, strength, wisdom and courage Lilly advanced further towards her ultimate goal with each doorway unlocking a deeper knowledge or an invaluable power that aided her in the upcoming trials. Onwards she went even as doubts were silenced by willpower allowing her to press until reaching the very end whereupon; buried beneath layers dust lay a treasure great beyond measure – Knowledge of all secrets known unveiled secrets unknown revealed mysteries once thought lost yet perhaps greatest secret uncovered during this perilous journey was unknowingly one discovered within herself had remained hidden since birth now appeared show way.

As Lilly stepped out from final chamber emerging surface victorious accomplishment rewarding tangible experience finally acquired realization true potential lies dormant within just waiting be found should follow courage heart never fear face one's own destiny no matter challenging path may seem because sometimes being brave means diving headfirst into darkness discover origin light itself, the truth seeking soul dwells deep rooted core person's essence deserving flourish bring radiance world through personal achievements attainments creating true sparkle life.

While stepping outside of the last chamber she was shocked to find a figure sprawled out in regal robes and ornate armor. It was Arthur, the King of Legend, long lost and forgotten, breathing slowly yet alive. Mystery unraveled before her eyes; a resurrection after years past.

Arthur's chest rose steadily as his blue gaze met Lilly's own wide-eyed stare; for once in control, feeling a sense of belonging, recognizing destiny written deep within soul, feeling drawn like moth flame towards him. She cautiously reached out to touch him, unsure of what to expect. As her delicate fingers brushed his armor, he smiled softly and weakly raised his arms towards Lilly welcoming her presence in this space between life and death, honoring the courage it took for one so small to make such an immense journey.

He said: well done, you completed your journey, you have done something that no one has ever done before. You can go back to your family but remember with power comes responsibility, don't forget lessons that you learned through your journey. Don't abuse your power and don't trust easily, farewell and he disappeared.

The grand library was quiet and chilling. She felt as if she was back in time, a century or two ago, here is a description of "Fate." It has fallen on many shoulders like a yoke pulling, always like a plow. It has fallen on those that are most yoked upon and strongest and they seem to carry it best.

Fate is a heavy burden that carries with it the responsibilities of life and its outcomes. It must be faced head-on, power through its will and taken on as one's own journey in order to see success. But even then, it comes with great struggle and no guarantee of victory - however small that may be, which keeps Lily motivated towards changing her grandfather's fate.

In determination to make a difference, Lilly took on passing her knowledge down through generations, for they should never forget what had happened before them or let another person fall into destitution under similar circumstances. With all she knew from

Merlin's teachings, Lily established an academy teaching young minds better ways than repeating old mistakes; letting hope reign over despair, recognition, kings long forgotten tales, walls filled with stories.

Lily's academy flourished as young minds were eager to learn and be inspired by the tales of great heroes and their conquests. With her determination and passion for teaching, Lily had created a thriving community.

The more she taught them about Merlin's teachings, the more they understood that fate was in their hands rather than some divine intervention or chance event. Their collective energy matched Lily's own understanding of destiny, it could be altered through sheer willpower. Like ripples on water, when one receives encouragement, hope becomes contagious, overcoming fear, doubt, despair just like fire brightening the cold dark room breath life into souls hopeless he brings moment peace before finally bring forth joy.

As years went by, even those beyond school age came to her seeking help in understanding how they too could fulfill what fate was destined for them. After many years spent improving others' lives with education, Lilly decided it was time to make amends with past regrets; especially where grandfather concerned.

She decides to go back to her parents; she was away from home for years, now grandfather was dead, and she raised so many students who understand magic, she could go back home.

As she arrived, her parents were beyond surprise and disbelief, tears streaming down their cheeks. They're usually stern faces radiant with joy that were impossible to contain; Lily felt like a piece of home had returned to them after so many years, absolutely nothing could compare. Her mother approached Lilly cautiously but with an embracing hug as if they hadn't seen each other for ages without any ulterior motive, just sheer unconditional love.

Her dad standing beside his wife beamed up at his daughter's eyes full of pride and admiration as he told Lily proudly "We knew you were special" even before she left it was clear now that he would do whatever it took to ensure her dreams come true no matter what the cost may be.

The family welcomed her back home reminiscing excitedly about all those days when she used to run around the house laughing the way only children can obviously worry troubles adults must face every day. They also shared fond memories of Grandfather that certainly weren't forgotten.

It seemed fate itself had brought Lilly here in an effort to recognize hard work, dedication moved by strength and determination Merlin taught; believing something better than destiny connected this wonderful young woman to return to the rightful place, making whole again.

She made the long journey into town, passing through villages along the way where people stopped what they're doing and gathered around. It seemed the whole world had changed since last seen here. A noticeably different present than the past showed recovery of nature's splendor, so she decided to go visit her grandfather's grave.

As she finally arrived at his gravesite, there were no words spoken but a solemn moment shared between two souls connected within deep hearts each found solace in silence. Here surrounded tombstones honoring those who had gone and rested under the beautiful canopy shade rose garden. Remembering the honor of life lived the sun glistened brightly, reflecting transpiring off distant lakes providing perfect mood contemplation remembrance, there was such a peace in that cemetery.

She wished fervently that her grandfather had never gone away. But looking at this place of peace, which he once occupied, brought her comfort too. She knew in some small way he will always be remembered here as well countless others now forgotten, lost life's battles. She branched out the academy and started teaching in her own hometown.

The people of her small town were equally surprised and overjoyed to see Lily once again. On hearing the news about her academy they all gathered in the local square together celebration held honoring. She was astonished with love and admiration showered upon. More than anything else appreciation for their own selflessness which gave way to Lily's bold endeavors shone during these festivities.

Lily had a positive impact on their small town; crime rates decreased as new students built homes creating families, bringing advancement knowledge breaking down walls of misconceptions between various faiths giving everyone a chance to understand each other. The legend of Lily spread everywhere who brought hope, peace into lives, illuminating darkness, spreading rays everywhere she went. Thus teaching the world "Hope is spirit eternal. It always prevails no matter what!"

The townspeople would tell tales of Lilly's past deeds and how she positively impacted their lives. They spoke of the young minds she inspired with her teachings, fostering a more unified culture while seeking to break down walls between different faiths and beliefs.

They praised her courage in having the strength to follow through on Merlin's words and make a difference in this world, which ultimately led to positive changes for all those around her. People shared inspirational stories about how Lily stood up bravely against an entire army that threatened peace among communities, always delivering messages filled with love instead of hate or fear. Her generosity was likewise uncontested as it seemed nothing could get past unwilling assistance.